S0-BXK-385

By Sherril Jaffe

This Flower Only Blooms Every Hundred Years (1979)
The Unexamined Wife (1983)
The Faces Reappear (1988)
Scars Make Your Body More Interesting and Other Stories (1989)

SHERRIL JAFFE

SCARS MAKE YOUR BODY MORE INTERESTING & OTHER STORIES

BLACK SPARROW PRESS • SANTA ROSA • 1989

This project is funded in part by the California Arts Council, a state agency. Any findings, opinions, or conclusions contained therein are not necessarily those of the California Arts Council.

Black Sparrow Press books are printed on acid-free paper.

Library of Congress Cataloging-in-Publication Data

Jaffe, Sherril, 1945-
Scars make your body more interesting and other stories / Sherril Jaffe.
p. cm.
ISBN 0-87685-780-2 (autographed) — ISBN 0-87685-779-9 (hard) — ISBN 0-87685-778-0 (pbk.)
I. Title.
PS3560.A314S29 1989
813'.54—dc20 89-27143
CIP

to the memory of Jackson Burgess

Table of Contents

SCARS MAKE YOUR BODY MORE INTERESTING

FROM THE WINDOW

SCARS MAKE YOUR BODY MORE INTERESTING

Over the Loudspeaker

"The heart is engaged at the moment, it will speak to you later."

"But the heart should always speak first, before the head."

"No, that is why we have a head. It will speak first, and it will consider the heart's wishes when the time is ripe. When we can work it into our schedule. Or, I admit, when the heart makes so much of a fuss that we are forced to listen."

"We are taught to respect the heart, and its tenderness. A cold heart is one which the head has neglected to plug in. When the heart speaks, the head sits back in the audience and looks uneasy. When the performance is over, the head picks the heart to pieces."

Accident

This accident happened to me because it was mere accident, just random chance.

This accident happened to me because, unbeknownst to me, I wanted it to happen.

This accident happened to me because it was fated to happen, by God, or by the stars, or by whatever.

This accident, which happened to me, was very bad, but it had to happen so that very good things could happen.

This accident has no meaning.

I will not discover the true meaning of this accident for a long time.

I will think I have discovered the true meaning, but it will not be the true meaning.

This accident didn't necessarily have to happen to me, but it did.

This accident didn't happen at all, it was my imagination. My mistake. This accident has been totally forgotten.

I just remembered this accident, and was sorry that I did.

Thinking about this accident all the time becomes obsessive.

This accident stands for something else not itself, in fact, it stands for a large number of things all of us experience—none of them itself.

The Bite

"This will feel like a mosquito bite," said the man in the white coat. She had a feeling that he was lying. She sensed that he was afraid to tell her what it really felt like. So he was tricking her, because then it would be easier for him. He would be able to get her to cooperate. He had no consideration for the way she felt about it. Now that she thought about it, she didn't even know what a mosquito bite felt like. She had never had a mosquito bite, or if she had, she couldn't remember. Later, when she was consciously aware of getting mosquito bites, she found that she didn't even know when the actual bite was taking place, but afterwards, on the place on her skin where the insect had bit her, a large welt formed which itched as bad as pain. The welt would develop pus and ooze, but she didn't know if the ooze was a natural part of the occurrence of the bite or an effect of the scratching, which, however she concentrated, she couldn't stop herself from doing.

But all this she discovered in the future. At the moment, all she could infer from what the man in the white coat and black hair was saying was that whatever he was going to do to her—and it was clear that nothing she could do could stop him—wouldn't hurt, and was, in fact, nothing to get excited about. But on the other hand, she knew that he was hiding something from her—the terrible truth of what he was actually going to do with her—and this was something which he had decided she was not to know ahead of time. But on the other hand, maybe he was straight. Why should she trust her own intuitions? The reasonable world was asking her to act reasonably. Perhaps she was acting like a child, doubting what everyone else accepted as a matter of course.

It didn't matter what she thought. And that was the final blow. As the man in the white coat was saying that this will feel just like a mosquito bite he was grabbing her index finger and forcing it down on a disguised needle which sprang forward suddenly and painfully, unlike any mosquito bite she had ever imagined or would ever again experience.

The Scar

It had been a large rabbit and it had bitten her sister on her index finger. Her sister had been rushed to the hospital. They had had to dispose of it. Ann had liked the rabbit. Now, no one else liked it. Ann was jealous of her sister for having been bitten by it, and thought, when she slammed the back door on her own index finger, that perhaps the rabbit had bitten her. That's what she told people who didn't know her sister. She did, after all, have a wavy scar on her index finger to prove it. Sometimes, if she petted it, the scar even ached, and that was enough to convince her that it was true.

After everyone seemed to forget, she went and got another rabbit. It was Easter time. This rabbit had something wrong with it. It couldn't bite her sister. It couldn't open its mouth wide enough. Never mind, she loved it. Sometimes, Ann bit her sister over the back seat at the drive-in movie. Now she was the rabbit. She knew they wanted to dispose of her, but of course they never let on. Her sister, being older, insisted upon being nice to her. Too nice. Ann sniffed at her food before tasting it to be sure her sister hadn't breathed on it. No one, of course, noticed what she was doing, and she, by this time, knew enough not to tell them.

For several years, the rabbit was her closest friend. Until her sister grew up and more or less went away. Until she replaced her sister with happier substitutes. Then the rabbit died. But not before she had stopped remembering to pet it.

Cause and Effect

When Ann played at Karen's they always played over at Laurel's when Laurel's mother wasn't home. One day they were playing over at Laurel's when Laurel's mother wasn't home and Karen decided that they should close all the blinds and take off all their clothes. So they closed all the blinds and took off all their clothes. Then they ran around the house naked. The only thing that put a damper on their fun was the thought that Laurel's mother might suddenly walk in, but perhaps this fear gave them even more fun. After a while, they put on all their clothes, and Karen and Ann went back to Karen's even before Laurel's mother came home. Ann was glad for this. She didn't want to see Laurel's mother.

That night, when she went home, she acted to her parents as if it had been an ordinary day. After a while she was put to bed, and she lay on her back in the dark. She lay there idly touching her chest under her pajamas. All of a sudden she felt something that surely wasn't there yesterday. She didn't know what it was. It scared her. It was like a large firm place under her nipple. Then she realized that she was just beginning to develop breasts. She suddenly felt very guilty about what she had done that day. She knew that had caused this.

She Thought

She wanted to give them what they wanted only if they found out they didn't want it when they got it. But they did want what they wanted when they got it, simply because they had wanted it. It was too simple to be logical. Her rationality had simply let her down again. Because she thought things out in her mind didn't mean, necessarily, that they really happened. When they did actually happen she was shocked and disturbed. She had figured that by thinking all the possible thoughts through to the end that *was* the end. She used thought like a charm to protect her from evil. If, for even a moment, she were to stop thinking, all the evil would creep in. But if the evil crept in anyway while she was thinking, then what was she to think? She could think anything, and several things yak yak yak filling up time. It was really like defensive talking—Well, all the children have died, and you are hopelessly infested with a very rare and grotesque tropical disease, but then, you know, not everyone can get such a disease blah blah blah everything happens for the best.

And that last thought, that evil Pangloss, obsessed her. It was—as she examined it she could see—it was a most comfortable thought. But it could never be proven until she was sure of what "the best" was. Of course, she knew what the best was, the best was entirely what she wanted.

Other people wanted her to want what *they* wanted. It was even true that other people worried that she wasn't getting what she wanted, or that she was wanting the wrong things. They even sometimes thought she shouldn't want what she wanted and definitely shouldn't get it. And when they *accepted* what she wanted and said "That's cool" to what she got she was sure they didn't care.

She had had her tonsils removed. Her throat was very dry. She was in a strange hospital. She had never been away from home before. She wanted a glass of water. She pushed the buzzer to call for the nurse. She had no idea what time it was. She was parched. The nurse wouldn't come. She rang and rang, for hours and hours. She didn't know why the nurse wouldn't come. Actually, she *did* know why the nurse wouldn't come. It was the middle of the night. The night was very long. The nurse came. "What do you want?" asked the nurse. She turned her head to the wall. "Oh, you wouldn't care anyway," she said. The nurse went away. Her throat was parched. She had no water. When the doctor came his name was Pangloss.

She had difficulty in asking people for what she wanted. Even when they said "That's cool" she couldn't believe them. Later she found out that the color red they had been both enjoying was actually mauve to him.

Sometimes, by accident, she wanted just what the others wanted.

Cat Chat

Ann sat on her bed for a long time looking at her cat, which was also sitting on the bed. From time to time the cat seemed to be looking at her. She wished that she could talk with the cat. How wonderful inter-species communication! She tried to talk with the cat first by speaking English. But this didn't work. She tried second to meow to the cat, to speak to the cat in its own language. But she couldn't tell if she were speaking real cat words, or if she were, she had no idea what she was saying, anyway. And she couldn't tell if the cat understood her, because she couldn't understand its response, or if there were any response. Lastly, she tried thinking towards the cat. But the cat didn't feel like talking.

Putting It on the Line

It was a mistake to deal in generalities. To deal in generalities was to beg the question, to find the easy way out the door, to put a blanket over your face. As if anything were *that* simple.

Nor did she believe in reduction to the merely personal. She wasn't going to make that mistake again. As it had been a mistake to cry while standing in the milk line with her six cents clenched in her hand, afraid that it wasn't the right amount, afraid that the big kids would ask her what she wanted when she reached the front of the line. And what *had* she actually supposed would happen?

And all those people in the restaurant—all those strangers—weren't really staring at *her* where she sat with her family. Her family certainly didn't notice. All they noticed was that she was taking things too personally. That was a mistake.

It had all been a mistake. A mistake to let *anyone* know that everyone in the restaurant was staring at her. Fortunately, that was all over now. She realized now that she was of the general wash of human beings, an inconspicuous fit at any dinner table. She was a person in general, and only herself in particular. It wasn't true, but there was no mistaking it.

And it enabled her to get on. To get on at all those endless dinner parties where no one in particular attended. And to chat in the most personal terms about things in general. Pass the salt. Not *my* salt. The salt you put on the soup, not, of course, the salt you rub in the wounds. There's no use crying over spilt milk. I know you don't really mean *me* when you say pass the salt, I know you're talking only about people in general, and not me at all when you complain how people never pass the salt anymore, and I agree, people are, in general, horribly inconsiderate, never thinking of others, and they all should be brought to the very head of the milk line where things are real and the real question cannot be anticipated.

And the milk line would go on forever, if you let it. Although there was no reason, really, why it should be there at all, except for general purposes of torture, and as a convenient method of putting things on the line.

Eating Her Heart Out

He was going to pick her up after school. She was to stand in front to meet him. They couldn't see each other every day—they didn't go to the same school. He was impressed by hers because it was the one the rich kids went to. She was impressed by his—he was the football hero at his school. She didn't know any football players at her own. There were always parties to go to at people's houses who went to his school. All people did at these parties was make out. The parties were always dark, and she could wear her new clothes which were better than the clothes people had at his school. The people at his school were impressed by her because she was the football hero's girlfriend. They would take her in their cars to his school's parking lot to cheer him when he got off the bus with huge bruised knuckles. She didn't understand football, but she pretended she did, and she pretended that it was exciting to her. There would always be a party afterwards where couples sat in dark corners french-kissing, and she suspected that other couples were petting, because she was. No one was fucking, but some of the girls had black boyfriends. None of the boys had black girlfriends.

He had a kindly face, unlike the dark sexy faces of the

other boys in their crowd, and his voice was somehow too high. He was always considerate and polite, however, but this probably wasn't tenderness. It was probably the idea of tenderness. In many ways, he was too sweet, but he had tremendously large hands scarred by football injuries. He gave her a heart-shaped box of chocolates for Valentine's Day. She despised boys who gave her presents. They were only doing it because they had seen people do it on TV.

She could barely stand to wait for her Civics class to be over. When it finally ended she hurried outside. She was wearing new clothes. They were very tight, and would have shown her body had she not been wearing a girdle and a bra. Everyone else was leaving the high school. They wanted to leave quickly as it was pouring rain. She stood in front looking for his car. After a while no more cars drove by. She felt disgraced. She thought he was standing her up. She had set, teased, and sprayed her hair because she knew she would see him that afternoon. She had spent a long time with her make-up. She was wearing perfume. But now she was wet. Her hair was curling and getting sticky. Her stockings were wet. He drove up, and she got in the car. She was furious with him, mostly because she looked terrible. But she didn't get mad at him to his face. He might see how awful she looked.

One night he picked her up to drive to the beach. She never really wanted to go to the beach because she knew her hair would curl up as it was always foggy at the beach. She didn't tell him she hated the beach because everyone else liked it. He had some beer in his car. She was afraid to drink beer because she was under twenty-one, but she drank it anyway. He was drinking a lot of beer, but he was the type who drank a quart of milk at each meal. When they got to the beach, they got down on the cold clammy sand and started to make out. Her bladder was too full, and she was glad when they left. On the way back they stopped at the first gas station because he wanted to pee. She wanted to pee, too, almost desperately, but she would never dream of letting him know. She sat in the car in front of the lavatory while he went in. With a shock of shame she saw that he was going in the wrong one! When he came out he got in the car as if nothing had happened.

When they drove up to the house they turned out the headlights as they came up the drive. Otherwise, they would shine in the windows of the rooms where her parents were sleeping. They sat for a few minutes in the car and made out. It was hard to do over the gearshift. Then he opened the car door for her, and she handed him the key to open the front door. She closed the door softly behind her and opened the door to her parents' room and said, "I'm home." They were lying awake in the dark waiting for her to come in. "Okay," they said. Then, presumably, they went to sleep. Then she tiptoed into the kitchen and slid open the bread drawer. And she ate whatever she could find.

Dimmi Quando Tu Verrai

They were staying at the Villa D'Este, the grand hotel on Lago di Como in that area of the world where Italy and Switzerland blend. It was the hotel where Mussolini hid away and was finally captured. It was his last resort. But it was more splendid than Mussolini, and more perpetual.

There were many waiters in the dining room, all so charming and seductive. The girls saved some of their rolls from lunch and went out on the verandah overlooking the lake and fed the fish with little pieces of the delectable bread. Then, in their bikinis, they swam out to the white boat that was anchored a few hundred feet out in the lake and sunned themselves on its bow. Pretty soon, some Italian men came rowing out to them playing their guitars. The girls pretended not to notice, but they were already in love—both of them with the handsome man in the boat. The other man was not so handsome. "Dimmi quando tu verrai? Dimmi quando quando quando?" the handsome man sang. "Weel you be at the dance tonight?" the men asked. The girls knew they shouldn't say anything, so they silently assented. Later, when the girls were dressing in their prettiest summer dresses, they went out on the balcony which overlooked the lake and looked for the rowboat. There was no one there. Then, while they were waiting for the dance to begin, they walked through the hotel gardens, through rose trees, and past other flowers which they didn't notice, singing "Dimmi quando tu verrai? Dimmi quando quando quando?"

The dance was beginning. Ann hoped that the handsome man would be there, that he would choose her. He was there. He was walking up to her to ask her to dance. He was offering her a Cinzano. But there was something terribly wrong. He was only about four and a half feet tall. She hadn't noticed this when she had seen him sitting down in the boat.

The next day as they got in the car someone came running up to her with a box of roses. It was the handsome man. The car door slammed. "I wonder whose garden those flowers were picked from?" her companion asked. All the way to Milano a bee buzzed annoyingly around the car. Ann knew she shouldn't be afraid of bees. When they got to the airport she left the flowers on a chair in the lobby.

Young Lust

He was hurting her, but she gathered from his demeanor that he thought he was giving her the greatest of pleasures. She couldn't tell him that he was hurting her because she didn't know, but she thought it might be supposed to hurt. She couldn't really take the chance of letting him know that she didn't know. Also, she was terrified of wounding his male ego. To do so would call forth the wrath of all the gods. It might mean that she would have to lose his respect. It would certainly be worse than the physical pain she was feeling.

If she said, "Ow! Cut it out!" as she wanted to, he would, of course, go limp. She didn't know this at the time however, but had instead a general sense that something unspeakable would happen. Then, perhaps out of anger, and perhaps by pure accident, she came. An unspecific and unfocused feeling flooded her. To describe what she felt in words such as "rivers of honey," and "the release of her soul into her streaming body" is hopeless. Then *he* erupted, and it was over. They lay in each other's arms, each comfortably alone, and safe at last.

After Capellanus

You really shouldn't want what you can get too easily. You should only want that which you might not get.

I want you. Or do I really just want the *getting* of you? Now I have you. What do I do next? That's the end.

But if the end comes, then, presumably, I want the getting of someone else. Or, if not, you do. At any rate, it's not easy. What is to be avoided is the easy attainment of the object.

I want you to come to my bower at midnight. I want to tiptoe to the casement. There will be moonlight, or the night will be very dark. I seem to want to wonder if you're really going to come, because I am wondering. I do want to spend a long time in my perfumed bath, however. And to dry myself at sunset when the light is rosy. I want to spend a long time with my hair, to pick my costume with infinite care, to spend a long time in contemplation of my own beauty. I am lost too far in anticipation to think how it will be when you actually hold me in your arms. I seem to want to study the clock, picturing you lost, wounded, dead. And I imagine that you have forgotten me, have not been possessed by dreams of me in the time we have been apart. I remember everything you said at our last meeting, and torture myself with what

I cannot remember, and what I can misunderstand. I am in terror that we are discovered, that the breeze is either too much or too light.

When you do come I am still not sure whether you love me completely and forever. There is no question but that I love you with all my heart, that I would sacrifice anything to be near you and to be loved by you.

Now I am sure that you do not love me at all, and that I am unworthy of your love. I will try to improve, or give myself up as hopeless.

Now I see that you are unworthy of my love and have become rather an embarrassment to me. Then there is also the problem of hurting your feelings. I don't want to have the responsibility of having to hurt your feelings. Moreover, I wouldn't want to make you unhappy. Because I care about you.

On Her Honor

He did her a great honor when he condescended to notice her. That meant that she could hold her head up high in the ranks of the world. It had nothing to do with a personal feeling he had for her, but rather, it had more to do with the idea he had of her. She also had this idea many times in front of the mirror, and so she was honored to receive it. This is not to say that the honor didn't change the idea she had had about *him*. It was clear to her that he deserved less honor than she had formerly given him. That the idea she had had of him before had been a mistake, a mistake in judgement. She now realized that he must be a fool. If not, why would he presume to think that she deserved so much honor? Of course, there was always a chance that she did deserve it all, and that there was no one she could look up higher to than herself.

How lonely it was. There was nowhere to go, nothing to do. There he was, way down there, looking up at her. She could barely hear him. Her mind wandered. She looked up at the blank expanse of sky.

Perhaps, however, he was neither a fool nor unhappily honest in his honoring of her. Perhaps he was using honor for some ulterior motive. Perhaps there was something he wanted from her, or something that he was afraid he would get from her if he didn't prevent it with honor.

He honored the privacy of her diary, for example. Or, another way of putting it might be that he didn't read her diary because he was afraid of getting a rude shock, of finding out what she really felt about him, really just how much she actually honored him. He honored the privacy of her diary, and he let her know that he did, that he never even felt slightly tempted to read it. That it never even crossed his mind to read it. In this way he made sure that she would never read *his* diary, that as soon as the idea crossed her mind she would feel dishonorable, and somehow dirty.

In another example, he paid homage to her achievements in the ranks of the world. She was someone he could look straight on at. Of course, that had to be. Would he waste all his energy looking down? No. That would make him lowly. So, naturally, he chose to look straight at her, and she looked back.

Needless to say, they were very happy. She knew she could trust him not to let her down, and she had promised not to let *him* down, for it wouldn't be honorable to do so.

After all, she did have a sense of her own personal honor. She knew when she should feel dishonored—that is, exactly how much could be done to her. And she knew just about how much she could do to others before she herself was dishonorable. To have it done to her was unbearable, but to do it to others was only shameful and embarrassing. In these cases she couldn't be expected to account for her actions. She could always look away from the poor person, look at another person, or a chair, for instance.

She was proud, of course, of the honor she did to others, but, in truth, she was more concerned about what was being done to her.

And he had done her a great honor. She had received a great tribute. She had been sitting in the audience with everyone else. On the stage, they were preparing to give out the honors. She wasn't paying any attention. These were boring occasions. Suddenly, she realized that her name, her own good name, had been called. She made her way out to the aisle and walked upon to the stage. There was a great silence coming from the stage as she walked towards it. When she got there at last they handed her honor to her. A few people talked about it and then they stopped. She took it home and put it on her desk. It was a token of something, surely.

Turning the Stem

When she turned the stem on her apple prior to eating to see who she was going to marry she always cheated. She didn't exactly cheat, but it seemed she could always get the stem to come out on the letter she wanted. She gave herself a scientific explanation. It was that the strength of her twist and the tenacity of the stem were a constant, so that every time she twisted she couldn't make the stem stick to the apple longer than the letter D. So she had to pick from men whose initials—either first or last—came from the very beginning of the alphabet.

These were not straightforward upfront men, necessarily. These were simply the men she happened to fall in love with. Any man in the latter part of the alphabet she happened to meet seemed to her like a persian. Actually, this was all a very dull cleverness, it was just an accident that the men in her life were all A's, B's, C's and D's. But were there A's? If not, that was because it was difficult to get the stem out on the first twist. But all this talk is a way to keep from actually biting into the apple, which sometimes is tart and crisp and other times spongy and flavorless.

She believed in divination by apples because it was

something she could control. And she could control the pleasure which apples gave by simple selection. But often she made bad decision—it was so difficult to make the right decision—and apples tricked her.

Grape Is to Raisin as Prune Is to What?

Ann had an interest in philosophy. She liked the logic part of philosophy. She liked the way logic could make things terribly true. She liked the way logic could discover things that were truth. She liked the way the forming and fulfilling of a relationship, a ratio, could discover truth. It was truth itself she was discovering, not simply the truth of that relationship. But Ann was also perverse. She did not believe in philosophy. She did not believe in logic. She knew some relationships could be fulfilled, and others could not. Finding the last piece in a ratio was an accident, in many ratios there was no last piece. No one else knew this.

No One's Filming

It was an existential movie, like smoking Gauloises while they sat drinking espresso in the Café Méditerranée. He had always been late, and even though she knew this, she was always ready on time. Then she would sit on her desk in her rose velour shirt, looking down eight floors, waiting for him to come. When he came, he was never in a hurry. What was the use? Everything was absurd. Then, in the summer, he came in his existential sports car and took her on a terrifying fast ride through the hills. She held on to her seat. He drove madly, but without true emotion. What was the use? They might die at any moment. Then he said, "I have another girl." She didn't know what to say to this, so she didn't say anything. "No one's filming, you know, Ann," he said. It was true. No one was filming.

The Mime

Nothing she had was her own but her white face.

Once He Had Kissed Me

Once he had kissed me, thousands of others were possible.

What She Stood For

Ann had known Karen in grammar school. She had been a cute little thing, like a kind of mascot. But now Karen had grown into a huge thing with a sober expression. Her hair was like a great pyramid. Ann couldn't accept this. To her, Karen must still be a mascot. Moreover, she was an emblem of the old days, the golden days of childhood. That is, she stood for the past, and Ann, who now had a boyfriend, wanted to show the past this boyfriend who stood for the attainment of all the desirable things of the future.

She never considered that Leonard might like Karen. How could he take a mascot seriously? Anyway, that would be too much like a corny movie. When Ann found out that Len did like Karen and was seeing her secretly she flew from equanimity into a rage. How could they do this to her? It wasn't what she had expected them to do. For some reason, they wanted to torment her by putting her inescapably into a boring movie.

Theoretically, she shouldn't have to care about the characters. It couldn't be that she cared, really, but she couldn't bear to be made part of such patterns which were tawdry fictions. Surely it was nothing personal, but somehow the archetype made her cry. It wasn't exactly that she had been a sucker. No, more grandly, it was that she had been betrayed. In essence, it was a matter of morals, and moral indignity. That was how she thought of it. That was how she chose to stand for it.

You Can't Teach an Old Dog New Tricks

When she had a bad experience, she chalked it up to experience. "Next time maybe you'll know better," they said. She thought that might be true. She would try to remember to try. But she would not remember. The thing would be upon her without warning. Suddenly, again. And she would do it wrong. She would then experience a bad experience. "Maybe you'll know better next time," they said. Why would they say that, to punish her? Didn't she already have her punishment when her experience went bad? "Maybe next time they'll think twice before saying it," she thought. But thinking was not really like that. Everything was suddenly underdescribed. She fell into a depression. Even though the bad experience was physically over it was still playing in her mind. She lay languidly on the nondescript couch and determined to change her life. She directed her future life from the couch in her living room. All the important details were there, and the smaller details, who were more important, were there, too. She put her hand on her forehead and watched herself have a better time of it, do a better job. *This* is the mind.

Later, when she was *out* of her mind, she went off into the world feeling pretty comfortable until she forgot what she had learned from experience. *That* was the mind, too.

Inevitably, she made some mistakes. When she was old all her mistakes were the same ones.

Her last mistake was a new one—she died.

She generally avoided thinking about death, but when she had to she could put it into a system—not heaven, quite, but a very high state. Why, loss of consciousness might free me for what else there is. She did not know what else there was. Her system did not always work. Actually, she was afraid to lose her mind. She did not mind so much losing her body, which was, although a great friend and a source of much satisfaction, often a chore. Moreover, her mind was her body.

That's all water under the bridge, now. And besides, the mind, and memory especially, is a funny thing. Things never are the way she remembers them. Things were, and instantly the past tense, like an enormous barrier, flees from the room. She only caught a glimpse. So her experiences might have been bad, but if memory is faulty, they were good. Or maybe if she had them right now they would be good. Such is constancy. She can have these experiences now, if you can really do things with your mind without your body along for support. She does have the experiences, but there is something missing. There is something empty about the experiences.

Something happens in the rest of the world which does not concern her.

His Girl

She looked forward to going to movies and parties and out to dinner with him, and being known by everybody as "Jack's girl." Was Jack his name? It would be a name with a complete personalized meaning once she got to know him, besides the generalized one she was hoping it also had. Hope had not been called for yet; she still had expectations. She expected to be somebody's girl soon, because she was nobody's baby now. This was the story of what happened to one, so therefore, she expected it to happen.

Jack was a person she had barely met at a party. She really did not know anything about him, but it was enough that he had asked for her phone number. She was a realist, she hadn't counted on him calling and asking for her address, and now he was coming over. What delight.

What delight while she took a bath. What thrilling momentary panic while she looked in her closet trying to make the right guess psychically in the multiple choice of what to wear which would be best suited to the occasion. He had not mentioned what the occasion was going to be. He had sounded gruff. She had not wanted to sound like a gold digger. So she had not found out where they were going—movie, party, dinner, which outfit would make her thinner.

And more attractive. She asked her roommates if she looked good, and sat down to wait. He was coming at the right time in her life. He could even have come a little earlier.

He was a little late. He was not very dressed up. First, she showed him into her room. She had no other place to receive gentleman callers, as she shared the apartment with two roommates, and one of them used the living room for a bedroom. She reached for her purse and jacket, and he lay down on the bed. He started to pull on her breasts. Before the natural law which governed the situation could even be registered in her mind. The natural law which governed the situation was that it was permissible, if there was no forethought, to allow a man to pull at her breasts but it could not occur before one had kissed him goodnight on the doorstep first. Surely this natural law registered somewhere in his mind. She gave him a little stiff caress as though to reassure him that everything was running smoothly, and started to reach for her wrap. But he pulled her down with his muscles and put his hand down her pants. Her attempts at conversation while she gently tried to shove his hand away were empty. By this time the law that no one can admit to being treated like this made her give him a big shove, which he could have overpowered if he had cared to. He spoke. "What's the matter with you?" he said. Was something the matter with her, then? He had convinced her that there was something the matter with her, but she would never admit it to him. No, she was not the person he had thought she was. She was instead a person with something the matter with her.

He wasn't sticking around to argue the point. He was getting up and tucking in his shirt as if she were no longer there. Maybe they were about to leave for the movies. No, he was heading for the door. She rushed after him to the door in order to be there showing him to it. He must have taken pity on her then. Why else would he tell her over his shoulder as he went down the steps to call him if she changed her mind?

She closed the door and turned around to face Bruce, who was eating a banana, but must have taken everything in. Bruce was her roommate's boyfriend's friend. And now he seemed to want to be her friend. Who was she that she suddenly needed a friend? She was somebody with something the matter with her.

"Take off all your clothes," Bruce said. "What?" "Take off all your clothes and stand on the bed," he said. His look assured her that she could trust him. She took off all her clothes and stood on the bed. "You're beautiful," Bruce said. "Thanks," she said. She did not know what else to say. This was not the right answer. "Say that you're beautiful," Bruce said. He was being very patient even though he had to repeat the command. "I'm beautiful," she said. She wondered if she should say that he was beautiful, too. Of course, he was completely clothed. But she sensed that this was not called for. There was nothing the matter with Bruce. She knew that she was not going to be Bruce's girl, either.

Come In, No Exit

She must have chosen to feel guilty about not doing the tedious thing she was avoiding because she had avoided doing that thing. Guilt, then, for her, must be easier to take than actually doing that thing (which actually wasn't too much to ask of a person). She could, after all, keep shoving the guilt to the back of her crowded mind, although she couldn't actually throw it out.

She decided to hire somebody to pull it out for her—everybody else was. Just before he started to pull, and as he was pulling, she could dissipate the feeling of guilt with crescendoes of excitement and activity which very nearly approximated relief. There was the chance that the person who pulled would be tainted with this guilt, but she didn't really feel guilty about this although she accepted the guilt of feeling responsible intellectually. Most of the time, however, she wallowed in the guilt, shoving it back when she was awake, and awakening it when she was asleep, dreaming. She found that she was growing sleepy earlier and earlier. If she was asleep she couldn't be expected to be doing that which she was avoiding, and she knew sleep was a good way of avoiding it. But she also made herself sleep so that she could let the guilt come forward. It was always pressuring to come out, and it found easy access in her dreams.

It wasn't that she was a masochist, of course, because she really didn't enjoy the torture. Yet, this didn't explain why she allowed herself to be tortured. Perhaps she needed a certain amount of torture at all times. This was most probably her parents' fault, or, more likely, the fault of the whole culture, which was, then, nobody's fault. Now that she had thought this she was no longer responsible. She no longer had to feel guilty about feeling guilty, or, more precisely, doing things or not doing things which insured that she would feel guilty. But she did feel guilty. She had made sure that she would.

In her mind she went on several excursions thinking things through, getting to the solution of the problem, facing up to facts, etc. This was another diversion she thought up to avoid getting to the solution, facing up to facts, etc.

In the end, when she got off the train of thought, she was back in the beginning, and the guilt, large as ever, was there waiting for her in the station. Although in the interim it had changed its clothes.

What could she do? She had to face up to things. She had to actually do the tedious thing, which, when she came to do it she would realize was no big deal. But there was no telling what she would be avoiding by facing up to it.

Trial and Error

Ann wanted to have friends. She had known people who had had no friends and she felt for them. She felt guilty about not befriending these people, but she couldn't bring herself to do it. These people were too hideous and unlikeable. So she did her best to hide the fact that she, too, was hideous and unlikeable to the people who became her friends. And they, for the most part, believed her disguise, so that eventually she became quite beautiful and charming. Everyone seemed to like her, so that eventually she had a husband and girlfriends and acquaintances. The husband, the girlfriends, and the acquaintances all had friends of their own, and these they introduced to her. Finally, she knew so many people that she was discovering that they all knew one another by one connection or another. She herself was more and more providing the connection. After a while, whenever she felt lonely, she could get one of these people to come over and visit her. They usually stayed, she found, longer than she wanted them to. The friends started to call up all the time and come over of their own accord.

In the old days, she had had a fear of being uncontrollably alone. If she were alone, she would have to befriend that hideous unlikeable girl. Now, she thought, she might like to meet her. At least, she was easy to be with. At least she didn't have to provide food and entertainment for her all the time. She might even get to get the dishes done before someone else drove up.

Then someone else drove up. It was Dick, a friend of Allen's whom she had met through Bev. He was good at doing takeoffs. He would do a takeoff on all her virtues. First, he would take off her tablecloth, and underneath would be the table. Actually, that was a small joke of his. Underneath would be the dinner, which would be all eaten up. Then he would eat away at her time. It was a trial of virtues, and if the trial went on for too long, she lost.

She tried to get comfortable in her hair while she listened to him neither making conversation nor leaving. He wasn't saying anything, so she had to talk. She talked about all the people who had been dropping in and eating up her time. He said he was leaving soon and started to do the countdown. She knew that her manners were bad, and felt a bit guilty about it. She knew she should out and out ask him to leave, but she was afraid to show her hideous side.

Then he was gone. She sat in front of the house quite alone for a minute, and then with horror she saw someone else driving up. This was someone she really wanted to see, but she still didn't want to see them. This was someone who was going away for a long time and had come over to say goodbye. She didn't want to see them. She started to sweat. She knew she should just reveal her hideous side and all this would stop happening to her. But she couldn't bring herself to do it. She wanted people to think well of her.

Dolce Far Niente

Ann rushed about cleaning the house. The sooner it was over the sooner it was done. As for the day, that was almost done, too, just a few splotches left. Ben came home and they went out to dinner, came home took off their jackets and he did his busy work while she wrapped up a hasty novel, and switching off the light, first she had a quick orgasm followed by his, almost before they rolled away they were asleep, woke up in the middle of the night for a bit of intimate conversation, slept and racing through dreams, up and breakfast and out the door, the sun bobbing up with a jerk over the streetcar and into the building. The days were getting shorter, and the nights were getting shorter, too, because it was that time of year, for a while, and then on to the next time. He kissed her, getting off the doorstep, then quickly splatted a shower on, rolled into bed just at that moment when the sun set and bobbed up again. She seemed to remember a different time, but didn't have time to remember, only that there was the same amount of time as there always was, only the parcels it came in now were jiffy-wrapped and the post office was always packed. So they hired more people, who had more children to mail more specials, and they signed here, and signed there, closing the door gently, this time, because at this point Ann resigned, and packed up the car, with Ben set neatly beside her all the way up to the mountain from which she never returned. It was cool up there, and they didn't know what to do with themselves after they got there and worshipped scenery for a bit, but it didn't matter much because after fifty years they were both dead and so the world ended, and at the end there was nothing, and God said the nothing was good, because by this time he would say anything just to pass the time.

A Young Boy and His Dog

Two years ago, when she was twenty-four, she got her first puppy. She walked over the hills with it. She pretended she was twelve years old—a young boy with his dog. Sometimes she knew the dog was only a prop—if anyone were to watch her taking her walks they would think there was nothing strange about it. They would think, simply, "Oh, a young boy and his dog." But at other times she knew that it was actually wonderfully true. She *was* walking through the hills with her dog, and it *was* real, as real as a movie.

The Meaning of Meaning

At first it was enough just to be alive. Then, everything would have been all right if the pain went away. Then, she wanted to feel comfortable. Then, it would have been enough if she had had something to do. Then she would have been satisfied if only she didn't have to do some of the things. Then she wished she didn't have to decide. Finally, a decision was reached. But she still wasn't satisfied. It wasn't enough. She wanted her life to have meaning.

Scars Make Your Body More Interesting

They lay by the side of the pool. "How did you get that scar?" Ann asked Emily. Emily explained with a titter of laughter. Then she said, "I have lots of scars. Scars make your body more interesting." Suddenly, Ann found Emily's body terribly interesting.

True to Life

She had never allowed the idea of having a baby to grow in her. When she went to the park and saw handsome young mothers playing with their pretty infants in the sand, she felt envious. When she met people who could never go anywhere or do anything because they had little children she felt safe. When she saw the extreme loveliness of children she felt deprived, and when children whose company she was forced to accept tried to take over her mind, to take over all her thoughts, to disallow her to have any thoughts which were purely her own, she felt righteously selfish. And resentful.

It was better in the long run that she didn't have children. Or was that just what she told herself because circumstances beyond her control would not allow her to have children? Or were the circumstances just an excuse for some larger but more hidden excuse? Perhaps she really *did* want to have children. She had no way of knowing. One way she used to find out was listening to other people, but other people were never quite as real to her as she was to herself. Perhaps that's what a baby was, someone else. But she had been a baby once, and she knew she wasn't real to her mother. Most people had babies, after a while, or wanted to. They told her she would want to have a baby when she found she was getting too old for it. She couldn't take this on faith. Everyone else had a baby, or was pregnant, and she felt left out, or free from it. There was also the fact that she wanted to be the baby, or be the child. Children could do anything they wanted to do. They could force their attention on anyone.

Other people's children often annoyed her. Sometimes she saw them throwing rocks at the windows of the room where she was to create her art. Sometimes they were noisy when she wanted to concentrate. Sometimes they were breaking her furniture, and making extra work for her who hated to do any housework. But sometimes children seduced her. Sometimes she had secrets with them, or could tickle them in their minds. Wasn't this enough, then? Did she have to actually produce one from her own body? Did she have to experience everything that it was possible for a woman to experience?

But any experience that she might ever have excluded other experiences, and to do something absolutely excludes not doing it. And having a child was forever, or for twenty years, which might as well be forever. And after twenty years it might be too late.

What would her child be like? Would it perfect all that she possibly could have been? Would her most hideous side be amplified, and mirrored up to her? She had no way of thinking about it at all, she said, and in this way she abnegated all responsibility. That thought, perhaps, was unfair to her. And saying that the reasons she remained childless were overdetermined said nothing, also. It was more jargon. Perhaps it wasn't thought only that kept her childless, but some force larger than herself, or some secret knowledge, or some strong intuition. It is possible that everything has an explanation, but it is equally true that things happen whether the explanations present themselves or not. And what happened was that nothing happened. She had no child, she didn't act. Why is it so fascinating to wonder why Hamlet doesn't act? But we can't let Hamlet alone, we can't forget him, because he gives no explanation that is finally satisfying. He is a character of limitless dimensions. We cannot judge him, we cannot say that he is not real, or that he is not true to life.

Swamped

As labor progresses, the cervix becomes thinner and more dilated. The membranes forming the bag of water rupture. The head molds to the shape of the pelvis as the baby gradually descends in the birth canal. Baby slowly rotates as descent continues.

She liked also to give suck. That was another reason to keep having babies. She had a distracted air about her, because all she was ever thinking about was nursing, and how she wanted some more. When she was actually doing it, an inward smile floated on her face. The size and shape of her breasts was indeterminate. She understood the whole reason for fucking, and was enjoying it for the first time. Dogs peed on her when she sat at the beach.

She was overcome by the fact of motherhood, and nothing else was real to her. Nothing else had any importance and she didn't bother to disguise this when she was with other people, or with her husband.

Their apartment was full of hanging curtains, dividing rooms and inside the rooms as curtains and canopies. Guests were always tripping on them. Her house was a cavern where there was no space unoccupied. There were piles of clothes and other things strewn about. The kitchen was large and sticky. She was always involved in strange combinations of natural foods which resembled the substances lining the inside of her womb.

Bolder

One way to deal with an obstacle which lies in your path is to remove it. But if you find after applying pressure that it will not give way—and there are, finally, those areas of life which will not yield—then the only thing to do is to add another obstacle: the new obstacle will significantly change the picture.

The Pattern

They had worked at having order so systematically, and for so long that it was impossible not to find order everywhere. He had been able to create a completely random pattern, but the result looked entirely orderly. This, of course, was just as he had expected, and it delighted him. Especially since he knew that no one would be able to tell that it was, in fact, purely random. That is, until he told them. When he told them was when he had his fun. That was not random. He had planned to show and tell them that their experience of order was an illusion, although unavoidable. Now that they knew his pattern was random they would have to use their imaginations to figure out what randomness felt like.

He told them that the whole universe was, in fact, random, even though they might have trouble realizing it. Perhaps they were afraid of it. It was unpredictable. They didn't know where they stood. Now they couldn't look forward to anything because there was no telling what was going to happen.

So the whole universe was out of control, not just out of their control, but out of all control. Even though they tidied up the kitchen so that it appeared that it wasn't there, the tidy kitchen was, he assured them, secretly an instance of randomness.

Did this make them feel less uneasy? Not necessarily. They looked at him doubtfully. It was, after all, difficult for them to accept the fact that they had been mistaken when they had thought his pattern an instance of orderliness, something he had planned. And it was even more difficult to believe that no one was in control, even if he did have his pattern to prove it.

Getting Pleasure Out of Cats

Dorothy was surprised and disappointed to discover that her neighbor's cat was just as versatile as her own. She had simply assumed that the neighbor cat must be ordinary. Before, she had thought that her own cat was far-out, but now she saw that it was no more far-out than the neighbor cat. Perhaps all cats were so. They probably were, she thought, out of her new cynicism. Then she went back to her own house and her cat jumped on her lap. She threw it off and looked away. Nothing the cat did could capture her attention. It was an ordinary everyday thing, and it bored her. She no longer understood why people kept cats, because it was obvious that none of them was special.

She looked at the cat with disgust. It was easy enough to blame the cat for tricking her into thinking that it was special by doing all kinds of cute tricks. It was only when she had seen the neighbor cat perform that she was able to see that the tricks were, indeed, tricks. She even felt vaguely embarrassed for her neighbor who seemed to get a lot of pleasure out of her cat.

Named After Me

It was a sea of glass and I awoke on the island, and the island had been named after me. It was a sandy beach, the palm trees were very high, just out of sight, and the branches rustled, but I couldn't hear them, they were out of my range. A coconut fell on my head and I spelled something wrong. "Come in, come in," the winds were whispering, and I whispered back, "I can't hear you, could you speak a little louder." Then the moon rose higher in the sky, and it was shining in my window, and in my window only, and I knew that the dawn had passed and I had been dreaming. The ocean was a mirror of glass, and the glass broke into infinite pieces, and we were adrift once more, endlessly reflected back upon our reflections. "Why isn't anyone steering?" I asked. "But there is no such thing as steering," they said. They said, "You've been dreaming, why don't you shut up and go back to sleep?" "Only to dream again?" I asked, but I could no longer hear their reply. "I don't want to play any more, " I dreamed, and it was named after me.

How He Made His Reputation

More than anything, Larry wanted to be famous. That was too obvious to everybody. He even acted as if he were famous already. Everyone talked about it, and how he tried to make an impression on them. They, of course, decided that they definitely weren't impressed. They all talked about him behind his back. But that didn't matter. Secretly, he was famous.

Already Trained

He admitted to them that he had gone to a prominent private university, but he added that he didn't like to tell people for fear that they would take him for what that means. He had gotten a job. It was a good job, but it was far from ideal, and it was what he had been trained for. He had gotten married, and it was a fine marriage, although it had been the prescribed course to take. He had gotten tenure, so he felt, with some anguish, that there was no choice but to buy a house. And besides, he now had a child. That had happened, as if by plan. Was this the end, then? He claimed to worry that he had come to the end, and wanted to search with real seriousness for some other end. All these facts of his life didn't necessarily add up to what they were supposed to. What did he take himself for?

This was the question he asked of them, who were almost total strangers, and knew only the broadest facts of his life. They thought that there must be some simple solution to his predicament, but they couldn't think of it just at the moment.

"Would you like a kitten?" they asked him.

"Thanks, but no thanks," he said. "When I do eventually get

a pet it's going to be a bird. And of course, I couldn't very well have a cat then."

"Oh, what kind of a bird?" they asked.

"What kind of a bird?" he repeated. "Why, I thought I'd get a parrot."

"Will you train it to talk?" they asked.

"Well, actually," he said, "that's why I haven't gotten one yet. I'm waiting to find one that's already trained."

A Critical Analysis

He was interested in literary criticism and could find several interpretations for "How do you do." It was obvious that "How do you do" meant more than what it seems to mean on the first reading. He thought for a few moments, and then he answered. "Fine, " he said. But that was, of course, not what he meant. Then he waited until the timing was right and asked, "How are you?" His companion knew what he was really asking, and they both smiled the smiles which give nothing away. They both delighted in this kind of repartee. At least he thought they did. He finally couldn't be sure of what his companion's smile stood for, for obviously, it stood for many things. Several possibilities suggested themselves to him, and he toyed with them in his mind. But then it suddenly came home to him what his companion had been driving at. He felt like a fool for not seeing it all before. Now he saw it all. It was all obvious. He promptly lost interest in the conversation.

A Clarification

She wanted to make herself clear. She wanted to make herself perfectly clear. She wanted to make herself absolutely clear. That is, she wanted her argument to be translucent. In fact, she wanted what she said to be transparent. She was trying to be lucid, to free her speech from turbidness. Moreover, she was trying to be both intelligible and consistent. She wanted, to be precise, to free her speech from obscurity. And to speak plainly, she didn't want there to be any doubt about what she was saying. In essence, she didn't want there to be any question about what she was saying. She was trying to make what she was saying perfectly plain. She was, that is, trying to make it evident. To put it another way, she didn't want to be misunderstood. And to put it another way, and perhaps a more significant way, she wanted to be understood. And it should be reiterated at this point that she wanted to be understood perfectly. She was striving to make herself clear to them, but it didn't matter, they had already seen right through her.

An Illegal Transaction

She bought the stuff and gave him an eight dollar bill. He didn't have change. All he had was a three.

Apology for a Sorry Case

"I'm sorry," she said. It was a trifling matter, but they were impressed by her politeness and good breeding.

"I'm really sorry," she said. Her manners were awfully good. Perhaps she overdid it a bit. They hadn't needed an apology.

"I'm so sorry," she said. They had been annoyed, but when they heard her plausible excuse they didn't see why she felt the need to apologize.

"I'm sorry," she said, but did this really make things right again? Wasn't it an empty gesture? If she was really sorry why did she let these things happen over and over?

She acknowledged that she was wrong, and expressed regret for the fault, which, she insisted, was her fault. But she wasn't without defense and justification. She knew the explanation. Did she really think that acknowledging that she was at fault did anything to amend the fault which she was at? Did she really think that getting things out in the open somehow made them go away? No, it brought them out in the open. It was really getting away with it to pretend that out in the open was as good as away.

She admitted that this was probably the case, and apologized for not seeing that before. They wondered if she really was sorry at all, or just said she was sorry in order not to arouse suspicion.

She apologized for making them suspicious, and didn't blame them if they got angry. Now she had made them angry. Perhaps this had been her intention all along, to make them angry to divert them from the fact of the thing she was sorry for. Or perhaps she had used the thing she was sorry for as an excuse for getting them angry. Perhaps what she really wanted was to get them angry. Perhaps she was glad they were angry.

No, she was sorry she had gotten them angry, she said. And she was sorry. Hadn't she been trying all along to tell them that she was sorry?

Then they saw that she *was* sorry, a sorry case. They regretted that they couldn't feel sorry for her, but she wouldn't hear of it. She had her pride. She wanted to feel sorry for herself.

Double Talk

A person who can do everything is a genius. All geniuses are mentally disturbed. Everyone knows that two heads are better than one. There are some things that seem impossible for you to do which are relatively simple for someone else. In a sense, that is why we are on earth—to help each other. But God helps those who help themselves. We are our own best friends, and we are our own worst enemies. For every good thing there is an equal and opposite bad thing. We must fight the enemy. No, we must not fight the enemy. We must turn the other cheek. All we really want is a little peace. No, we want complete peace. And this peace has to be insured. Someone has to be on guard. Someone has to be the social secretary. Someone has to get something done. Someone has to do the disturbing things so that there will be some meaning to my peace. I don't pretend to be a genius, and my personality is well balanced. Because I put half the work out for hire and I got the job. This was not to sell myself short, but to double my chances.

Forgotten Object

Every time she went to someone's house she left something behind. Every time she got a ride in someone's car she forgot something. Every time she hitched a ride something remained in the car after she had left it. She had to leave the house, she had to leave the car. That was going completely. But if she left something behind, that was not going quite completely. Soon she would be back.

She didn't like to think of them all back at the house continuing without her. They should stop now, now that she is gone. Frozen in their chairs. Even the clock has stopped.

It wasn't necessarily desirable to be everywhere at once. If she were, then no one would miss her. And it was important that they should miss her. At first, they were annoyed when they found her glasses under the table. Then they wondered when she would come and get them. Every day they looked at her glasses and thought of her. Then she came and took her glasses away. But she left her checkbook behind.

Now she saw where she was going, but she couldn't pay for it. Although she had to pay for it in the end. Or she would have to pay for it when she got back to it, where it all started. She was making her way back slowly, like walking upstream, from forgotten object to forgotten object. Mathematically, there was no way she would ever get to the end. But she had forgotten all her mathematics.

Who She Was

She was a body all of salt. She was told that she was Lot's wife just as others had told her that she was Madame Bovary or Piper Laurie. The one who had told her she was Piper Laurie was wrong. Or she assumed she was wrong, not knowing, really, who this Piper Laurie was, except that she probably had freckles and was an unromantic film star. But the men had all made her into wives, wives whose lives were tortured by turning away from their husbands.

The Separate Life

When he comes home from work she comes to greet him pretty as a picture. The dinner is all made, and there is no mess in the kitchen. She smiles gently and jokes away his trials of the day. Later, he receives a phone call, and she can tell from his expression that it is a serious one. "I have to go out," he says to her. She can tell from his expression that he has to go out on a dangerous mission, but also that she must not show her fear to him. Her expression now is serious. But it is still understanding. Even though, of course, she doesn't understand. She only appears in two scenes of the movie. She has no separate life.

Getting It Out

As soon as she met him she didn't desire him. It was just that it never crossed her mind. Because it would be a complication, a disturbance of the natural order, the easy order of things which was difficult enough as it was, anyway. So she got to know him unintentionally. She knew that she took pleasure in his company.

She was surprised for many reasons when he suddenly kissed her. She was surprised that he did it. She was surprised that she liked it. She was surprised that the possibility of further embraces was created and surprised that the possibility might always have been there. She was confounded, and couldn't think about it, but could only dream about it driving alone in the car or lying alone in her body at night.

But there were, after all, other people involved. And she had to think about it when they all talked it out. So she thought it out, and the other people helped her. Get it all out, they said. So she did, and they got it all out. They got it all out in the open. That was how they got it to go out.

Proof of Friendship

Ann was being asked to prove her friendship, and so, she no longer felt friendly. Connie was looking up at her beseechingly. Ann was sitting on the table looking down. She hadn't intended to do so, but it was significant. Connie said, "I just wanted to know how you felt about us. I helped you paint your house, and you promised me that you would help me paint mine. And when you didn't, I thought it was a little strange. I didn't want to bring it up, I just wanted to know how you felt about us." But why doesn't she want to bring it up? Ann thought. It seems pretty clear evidence. Why if I were her, I would hate me. Maybe Connie thought it was too petty to mention it. Ann certainly wasn't going to tell her that it wasn't petty. Then she would have to admit out loud that she had done something petty, something selfish and dishonorable, as she had. In her heart, which must be very cold, Ann was forced to relive in emotion the shame she had already felt at letting her friend down. She knew she had given her friend pain and worry, but somehow, her heart didn't melt towards this friend who, in all fairness, deserved to be told that she had been a true martyr, that she had been slighted but that there was some highly plausible excuse which she could just believe, and that Ann treasured their friendship to such a degree that she would suffer backwards, would bend over backwards to suffer as much as her friend had been made to suffer and more.

But just at that moment Ann didn't feel like suffering. She did not even feel like suffering the pain of speaking her mind and telling the friend to go away, that she certainly didn't like her at the moment. She would have to think about it. To wait and see if she missed the friend at all. She could see that her friend didn't want to bring up the nasty reminder of Ann's temporary irresponsibility and thus that the friend was of true and unselfish character, and was, indeed, invaluable as a friend. But Ann could also see that the friend was dying to throw proof of Ann's nasty behavior in her face, because that is, after all, what she had done. And she got to do it without having to admit that she *wanted* to do it. She had got to do it and not to do it at the same time. Ann thought she was getting entirely too much. That she shouldn't be allowed to have everything. That a true martyr must sacrifice something. Ann knew then that they could never be friends, because she was obviously not worthy of her.

Beyond Repair

The first time he met her he imagined fucking her. But then, all women, except for a few obvious disasters, he considered so. He could appreciate many things about her—the luxuriance of her body hair, for example, not to mention the terrific possibility that she was attracted to him. And he was enamored of the whole mystery that encompassed everything that he didn't know about her, and therefore, everything that she possibly could be.

It was true that he was still concurrently in love with his wife, but there was nothing he could do about his passion, as he explained it. He and his wife discussed the problem, and they couldn't come to any satisfactory solution. His wife was afraid that she would be left out, but didn't see any solution which enabled everyone to be included. They both talked about it with the other woman, and the other woman talked about it alone with his wife. They talked and talked and talked. The intensity grew and the intensity of the love the wife bore the husband grew, as did his for her. The sexual pleasure they took with each other grew to the very heights which passion can engender. And they were still talking, so that nothing could happen between the husband and the other woman.

The man began to see faults in the other woman. He began to discern her limitations. Her biggest fault was that she was indiscreet, and had to do, as it seemed to him, with other men who were unworthy of her favors. It was a fault in her which annoyed him, not only because he was not the only special man in her life, but because he never could be because of her faults which, of course, had nothing to do with his real specialness. It was a pity he hadn't fucked her before he had found all this out and before all the talking had begun.

He decided he didn't want to see her anymore. If he saw her, he wouldn't be able to stop himself from wanting to fuck her which he wouldn't be able to do as at the same time he wouldn't be able to disregard her faults, which he had assessed as beyond repair.

He stopped seeing her quite suddenly. At the same time, his love and passion for his wife dwindled, as did hers for him. This was only a temporary setback, however, for their love soon began to grow again. But would it never end?

The Age of Enlightenment

Martha didn't have to want to possess Harvey to want to sleep with him. It was just that people were, as she said, "polymorphous perverse," so it was only natural that she should want to sleep with him. And meet his wife. Women were as interesting as men. She knew that. And when she told him that she wanted to meet his wife he smiled warmly. Of course—it was the age of enlightenment after all. Why shouldn't his wife and his mistress be friends? It was only natural.

One day, when Martha hadn't seen Harvey for a while, she called up and said she would like to come for a visit. "Sure," he said. "We're home." Oh, so his wife is there, she thought. All the better. When she arrived his wife was just finishing the dishes. She wiped her hands and smiled warmly. It was probably a warm smile, but Martha couldn't be sure because she had never met Harvey's wife before. Martha had a headache, and understandably, for it had been a long drive, so she asked for some aspirin. His wife was very solicitous, and offered her not only aspirin, but several other helpful drugs.

Harvey's wife was very talkative and made every one in the

room laugh with her stories. Martha knew that his wife was entertaining, but she couldn't quite laugh. Perhaps it was the drugs she had taken. Harvey wasn't talking to either of them, it was better that they be left alone to get to know each other. In fact, he could hardly bear the situation, and couldn't really talk to anyone. He talked to the plants in the corner instead.

They all decided to take a stroll. Harvey and his wife went through a ritual of getting ready. Martha recognized that it was a well-known ritual to them. They seemed to like to take strolls. While they were strolling, Harvey strolled slightly ahead leading the way. Martha and his wife strolled together, chatting. His wife pointed out all the sights to her. The sights were wonderful. Unfortunately, Martha couldn't give them her full attention, as she was distracted by the fact that her nose was running. She must be allergic to something in the atmosphere. Why was his wife talking about birds of prey, anyway?

When they got back to the house Martha asked whether anyone else found it damp? "Why, I guess it is," Harvey's wife said. Apparently, she had never noticed that it was damp before. Martha knew that it was damp because her back ached. Harvey's wife offered her something for it, but she refused, saying, "No, I'd better not take anything, it might make me sleepy and I have to drive all the way back, and I'll be all right as soon as I get out of here anyway, thanks anyway." "Oh, are you leaving so soon?" his wife asked. "Yes," Martha said. "I have a back ache."

Harvey followed her as she walked out to her car because he wanted to know if there was anything the matter. "Oh, no," she said, as he kissed her deeply. Not that he had to sneak a kiss while his wife wasn't looking. It was, after all, the age of enlightenment.

Extra-Marital Relations

If the husband goes out alone at night the wife does not sleep but watches for him anxiously. When the time draws on and it is near morning, then she knows "he has gone to the women." When he returns he thinks she is asleep, but no, she is waiting for him. She has a stick with which she bangs him on the back of the legs, and she pinches his flesh until the skin is broken. This he must suffer as quietly as he can, in order not to arouse suspicion.

In My Role

In my role as a dwarf in a sideshow I was invulnerable. Yet, I admit, the pay was not good.

Alone At Last

She was alone, so she went into the bedroom to try to seduce herself. She stood in front of the mirror. Her face needed washing, so she went in and washed it. There was another mirror over the sink, but she didn't look in that one, she didn't look good in that one. She went back in the bedroom. That tee shirt wasn't right, she put on a nightgown. Now her hair was messed up. She started to brush it, and looked at herself critically while she was doing it. Now it looked all right. She smiled. Then she looked at her smile from one side by looking into a hand-mirror at her reflection in the big mirror. Now she looked at her smile from the other side. Then from above, then from below. Then she tried a serious expression. That made her face look quite beautiful. She wondered how that serious expression looked in bed, spread out across a pillow. She held it in the mirror while she backed towards the bed, pulling her socks off with her toes. Now she was in bed, looking at the serious expression very close. She wondered how it looked with its eyes closed. She closed her eyes and she went away. She was alone once more.

The Soft Ku-kuh

The car was very relaxing. The back seat was very soft. As they rolled along they heard the car make a soft ku-kuh sound, over and over. It was not the motor. The motor was in good shape. It had not always been in that car. It had been in another car which was no longer there. The soft ku-kuh was not in the road. The road did not make any sound. The soft ku-kuh was the universal joint gradually breaking apart. Soon the motor would be in another car.

Beyond the Pale

"Oh, Ben!" said the voice coming out of the phone. "We did hear you were in town, and really, we *had* meant to call you!" Ann could hear the voice in the phone clearly from the other side of the room. It was projecting. Ann knew that Flora, this voice, was an actress. That's how come Ben had known her when he used to live here. Ann knew that Ben used to act. But she had never seen him perform.

This voice did not sound unprepared for Ben's phone call. It sounded rich, full, clear, and whether or not it was sarcastic was ambiguous as only the best playwrights can describe.

Yes, the voice did seem ready with really urgent questions. "Oh, Ben!" it said, with compassion welling up. "Really! How can you *bear* to live in A*mer*ica? I mean, with all those Americans?" It asked this with real concern and pity, and a touch of monomania. Ann was surprised. What a crude kind of nationalism some of these Canadians have, she thought to herself. Where I come from no one has any interest in such gross concerns as nationalism. Everybody *is* American. Ann said this to herself, because she couldn't very well say it to Dan Daniels, their host here in Canada. Anyway, she didn't want to miss Ben's reply.

"Well, I'm married to one now," Ben replied into the phone. Ann realized that he was talking about *her*. So she was being introduced to Flora, this voice, as "one." One American. One of them. "Well, it's all settled. We're going over there," Ben said as he hung up the phone.

"I really gave it back to Flora when she gave me that bit about Americans, didn't I?" he said, chuckling. Ann chuckled, too. So it had been a great come-back, and not an insult to her at all. She didn't understand exactly how this was so, but after all, *she* didn't pretend to know anything about acting.

Dan Daniels decided to go with them. He had met Flora in the old days, and thought it would be amusing to witness the reunion of Ben and Flora, although he did not act, either.

On the way over in the car Ben told Ann and Dan that he was sure that Flora didn't want them to come over, and that was why he was determined to go. Ann wondered if this was a Canadian custom or an actor's custom. Ben was talking as if this was a sort of boxing match, and he had won round one. Well, if this was going to be a boxing match, Ann promised herself not to fall down in the ring. But why should she fall down in the ring? She knew that actually there was no ring. These people had nothing on her.

They were greeted at the door by Flora's husband, Boris. Boris greeted them effusively, but Ann knew he was an actor. He was wearing a purple cardigan sweater buttoned over a purple shirt. Ann had seen many men wearing cardigan sweaters buttoned over shirts since she had arrived in Canada, but none of them had been purple. The purple of Boris's costume, Ann deduced, showed how unique and avant garde he was. It must be the flag of his art, she thought.

They were shown into a room and Ann was offered a very uncomfortable chair. As Ann looked around the room she thought how comfort and decorating must be only things of this world, and not any part of that higher world, the world of great art which these people represented. There were two other women in the room and a sort of man draped across an easy chair. Dan Daniels whispered to Ann that this was Edgar, a really great actor. A little brown beer bottle appeared before Ann.

Everyone in the room was holding a little brown beer bottle. Dan Daniels whispered to Ann that everyone in Vancouver was holding a little brown beer bottle just at that moment.

"Oh!" Boris cried, shocked at himself for forgetting his manners. "Would you rather have a glass? . . . Uh?" "No," Ann assured him. She didn't need a glass. Why should she be supposed to need a glass when no one else needed a glass? Because she was American, or because she was not an actress? Actually, she didn't even like beer, but she wasn't going to give Boris that satisfaction. And she wasn't going to acknowledge that she had noticed that Boris had forgotten her name, either. Ann felt that she was holding her own. She looked around to see if Ben had noticed and was proud of her.

But Ben was now talking to Flora who was pointing out to him very kindly how his life must be a misery since he had moved away. Ben was saying, "Well, actually . . ." and the woman sitting next to Flora was looking at Ben with pity. "That's Nora—she's married to Edgar," Dan Daniels whispered in Ann's ear. Ann looked at Edgar again. He hadn't moved. He looked debonairly bored. Or perhaps he was dead, and preserved in wax.

"And *who* did you say you were?" Boris inquired of Dan Daniels. "Dan Daniels," Dan Daniels said. "Ah! Daniels," Boris said. "And what did you say your first name was?" "Dan," Dan Daniels said, adding that they had met in the old days, but he didn't expect Boris to remember as he had never acted, but just at that moment Boris was forced to stop listening to him because he had just reached the reasonable limit of his tolerance. "Flora!" Boris screamed. "Flora, I *really* think you're being terribly rude! I think you've got to acknowledge that rudeness like this is beyond the pale of common humanity!"

Ann had not noticed until now that Flora was being rude. She had seen that Flora was chatting quietly with Nora. But now she saw that Flora was purposefully cutting the rest of them out. All eyes, except Edgar's, turned to Flora, who looked deeply hurt and wronged.

But very patiently and deliberately she replied to Boris's outburst. "Nora and I were only talking about our children," she said. "If two mothers can't talk about their children, well I don't know!" "Yes, if two mothers can't talk about their children, well I don't know," Nora added, as if to ask if the world were really such a sad place. In the dead silence that ensued, Ann heard a banging and thumping from the floor upstairs. Apparently, this was children. Then Boris screamed, "But I have to insist. *Ben* is here!"

All eyes turned on Ben, except Edgar's, which gazed beyond the veil, or into the curtain. Ben cleared his throat and started to talk about his new life—what he was doing, the concerns that had become important to him. He paused, and no one said anything. Then Boris spoke. *He,* at least, felt *his* sense of decent social obligation. "I really do think Ben's voice has become more resonant," he said. Flora's face slowly lit up. "Oh, yes! More resonant!" she said, smiling now, almost laughing. Then she turned back to Nora and they started to pick up where they had left off.

Ann saw that Ben was looking around for more beer. "You can have mine," she said to him. Then suddenly Flora was addressing her, Ann. Ann had not known that Flora knew she was there. "Oh we're not going to get into a deadly dull feminist debate, now, are we?" Flora was asking her. "What?" Ann said. She turned to Ben, but she couldn't catch his eye.

"Oh, no!" Flora cried, as if she could hardly believe it, but it was giving her a headache, "You're not going to have a scene now, are you?" The back of her hand was raised to her forehead as if in defense, and Ann was going to reassure her that this was not necessary, but she was back talking with Nora again. "Really, I must insist!" Boris protested, and Ann got up to find the bathroom.

But Flora was after her down the hallway. She took Ann by the hand. "We're not really so awful as we seem," she confided. "Oh, I don't think you're awful at all," Ann said. She wasn't going to give Flora that satisfaction. Flora indicated the bathroom. "If you find any little children in there," she said tenderly, "just shoo them out." Her voice was choked with emotion. When Ann came back in the room Flora was talking seriously to Edgar about her next role. Ann wondered when Edgar would speak and reveal to everybody that his next role was in a wax museum. Ben was explaining to Nora and Boris and Dan Daniels about his life, his daily concerns, how he enjoyed talking. Flora and Edgar drifted into the other room. Soon Ann noticed that Nora was gone, too. Ben continued talking—about the floorplan of his house, his garden, the place where he worked, things that had been in the paper recently. Ann saw Flora showing Nora and Edgar to the door. They had their coats on and two waxen children. Then Boris disappeared. Apparently, he had gone to the bathroom. After a while, Flora came back in the room and curled up upside down in Edgar's chair and went to sleep. Ben continued talking to Dan Daniels, about the general problems which present themselves in everyday life, how different people he knew dealt with them, and possible theories. Ann noticed that Boris was not returning from the bathroom. Flora was snoring. Ann wondered if this was real proof of the confidence of a great actress, that she could trust herself to sleep in front of her audience, would trust that she would give the right impression while asleep.

Then Flora's snores suddenly ceased, and she was laughing

uproariously. "Oh, Ben! You don't really believe that!" she laughed as she stood up and walked out of the room. They could hear her laughter as it went up the stairs. It was dead silent for a minute while the three of them left realized that Flora had gone to bed. Then Ben started up again, talking to Dan Daniels, telling him about things he had begun to be concerned with lately, how people continually miss the point.

"Why don't we go home?" Ann asked. Ben was apparently unperturbed that his hosts had gone to bed. Ann was glad that Ben didn't seem to be insulted by Flora and Boris. If Ben didn't seem to be insulted, perhaps they had not really been insulted. After all, Ben knew these people better than Ann did. He had performed with them. She waited by the car with Dan Daniels while Ben peed against the side of the house.

Part of the Picture

When Ann took her dog for a walk, the dog peed on everything. When they got to the forest he peed on every bush. At the end of the forest he peed on the last tree. This was his last message.

Downtown, now, they went first to the post office. There was a face in the window to help them with scales and handling. Ann looked through the window to the inside of the post office, which could be glimpsed, but never probed deeply.

Then Ann went into a phone booth alone. Her dog wouldn't fit. Even though the door had been ripped off. In essence, she was right on the street making her phone call. It was a serious phone call she had to make, it was about a serious matter. She must convey the seriousness of the matter to the party she was calling, without telling them more than they needed to know.

She was doing very well. No one was listening. She accomplished her mission and the problem was resolved. They walked back through the forest. The dog wanted to sniff everything in the forest. He was telling himself a story. He could tell what had occurred on that spot at a time in the past by sniffing with his nose, and turning his eyes inward.

Every time he sniffed, Ann stopped. She was taking him for a walk in part of the picture.

Every Cloud

I used to have a full set of silverware, but when I went to set the table the other day I was dismayed to find that many of the pieces were gone. I am telling you this so that if you have been carelessly taking forks or knives out of the house and then carelessly throwing them away or leaving them somewhere unthinkingly you'll now realize that I care if my silverware melts away and take more care in the future. Of course, I'm sure that you know nothing at all about it and don't even know what I'm talking about. That's as unlikely as the idea that you may be starting your own silverware collection! But I know you wouldn't be interested in a thing like that. I'm sure you just take silverware for granted. But let me tell you, it just doesn't come out of nowhere. So then where does it go? Not that that's the point. And I don't want to put a cloud over our relationship. All that matters to me is that there be a reliable amount of silverware. Perhaps if I check in the drawer after a while I will find that some of it has replenished itself. As is so often the way with things that cannot be kept track of. Then I will not have to be always thinking about silverware. Like you.

Making New Starts

It was nice to think that she was making new starts but really what she was doing was starting over. Like going out and then coming back because her car was blocked. Then going out and getting the person to move the car. Then going out and coming back because she had forgotten her purse. Then coming back anyway because the car wouldn't start. It was obvious that what she needed to do was to make some new starts in her life. She would start over. This time, she would be a better baby. Her childhood would be innocent. She would pick loveable parents.

"Yes," said her husband. "It is apparent that in me you find a loveable parent, but I am not your father, why don't you grow up?" Yes, he was right, it was high time that she grew up. She would start on it right away. "Oh no," he said, "now you are the mommy, I don't think that's really grown-up, Mommy, always to want to be the mommy." It was just a game she had started, anyway. She took off the fox-fur and sat down. "I'm going to start in a minute," she protested to herself. "I'm just resting for a bit. Just catching my breath. It's just that starting is the hardest part. Because there's a bigger difference between not having started and starting than there is between actually starting and imagining finishing. Because that is all you imagine once you start, you imagine finishing. You never imagine starting over."

But you have to start sometime, she knew, so she put the fox-fur back on and started out on foot. She had heard people talk about taking a new lease on life, and turning over a new leaf and felt she should gain courage from such propositions which, after all, were everywhere in the world. It was hard going, walking, and she didn't know where she was going. Never mind, she had started, so she had better finish. That was the grown-up thing to do.

She felt better now, just walking along, starting down the road towards something or other. Well, she would see when she got there. She had started and there was no turning back now. Late in the day she got there. It was the wrong place, so she started out again. She got there just as night was falling. She was tired, and she sat down. She had some supper and she went to sleep. These actions were soon completed once they were started. She woke up and was startled to discover that it was a new day. For every day is a new day and promises a fresh start.

Voice Prints

When Connie called Ann on the phone, she had no trouble in recognizing her voice, and thus recognizing that it was Connie who was calling her and not Dorothy. That is because Connie's voice is different from Dorothy's. In fact, no two voices are exactly alike. Every voice is different. No two people are exactly alike. Each person is absolutely individual. How varied human being! How astonishingly different each individual! This is very significant information. It is significant, for example, to the telephone company and to the F.B.I. If we were all the same we would be safe from the F.B.I., unless we were mistaken for someone else.

On the Proper Content of Conversation

It was better that everyone didn't talk about politics and religion, although there was also the fear that someone would. One had to be prepared for such eventualities. One had to be prepared to pretend that one was a little deaf, or to simply agree with whatever the person was saying, although in a strictly mild and noncommittal way—Yes it is really a shame that the massacre had to happen, but then no government, not even the government of God, is perfect. Yes, one had to constantly be on one's guard. There was always the possibility that there would be a person in the room with some secret religion or political belief. It was not like talking about the color of someone's socks, socks never seriously reveal a person, but rather are useful in the covering up of the feet and legs, whereas a person's political persuasions immediately give him away. In the realm of politics it is clear as a comic book what is godlike behavior as it is clear what is evil intent. So it is clear if a person affiliates himself to what is dastardly, that he himself is dastardly to the embarrassment of all present. Although from the bastard's point of view, his reasons are more sound than insane, that is, they have to do with real things, the hard facts of things, such as property, or his own feelings of justice. And he may persist in insisting that everyone agree with him, or at least that they should disagree with him. That is the time when you should pour the tea, because if you should slip, be caught off guard, you might be tricked into saying what you really think. Your stockings would, as it were, fall down, and as everyone got up to go you would say well, fuck it, those are my legs, and I've had them all along. Then everyone would leave and they might not come back. And you would no longer be able to pass such pleasant evenings as this.

But we know that is all wrong now, for we have lived in the past. And now we are in the present where we know that no one will admit to being offended if we talk about everything, because, although legs in general have tremendous significance, yours are, after all, only yours. We are frank now, and will talk about anything. After all, we have been talking for a long time now and I know your legs backwards and forwards. And we all agree about legs, every leg is just fine. There are no religions left that aren't both ridiculous and groovy. We can accept it all.

And it is important now that we do not waste our time together, two or more, the more the merrier, human beings communing, but get right down to the meat of the matter. And it is all very important, just as nothing we ever talked about before ever was. We know now how important it is to say things just as we knew in the past how important it was not to say them. How clear is truth and how easy to say it.

Cigars Make Your Body More Interesting

Ann might have been really fascinated by mushrooms—not real mushrooms, but the animated or facsimile kind of mushroom—or she could have wanted people to think so. When she drew, it was often the picture of a tortured person of indeterminate sex with a mushroom growing on his shoulder. These might have been drawings done to horrify or shock people, wasn't it cute, or they could simply be art. She had things in her apartment which were in the shape of mushrooms. Some people laughed when she brought mushrooms up in the conversation. Or when they saw the things made to look like mushrooms in her apartment. It was obvious that a mushroom was a phallic symbol, and that what she had were phallic symbols displayed all over her apartment and in her pen when she drew. This was all a set-up on Ann's part. "That's what *you* think, *Mr.* Freud," she said. "But did you ever ask yourself what a phallus is a symbol for? No." But she let people see phallic symbols instead of the mushrooms that were really there. But when people tried to humor her in her fetish, giving her little banks in the shape of mushrooms and mushroom salt-shakers she realized that she had lost interest in mushrooms. Now, when she went into stores, she saw mushroom everythings on sale. Mushroom candles and mushroom placemats. People's personal stationery began to have a mushroom design. Everybody had suddenly just discovered mushrooms. Ann had known mushrooms before anybody had thought of it. Most people did not know this fact about Ann. Most people had never even heard of Ann. Now they had all discovered mushrooms, but it was too late. Mushrooms were no longer interesting.

What was interesting now was airplanes. Airplanes which did skywriting out of a very pubic part of their anatomy. Although they were of indeterminate sex. People wonder what this airplane is supposed to represent, and they think they know. Ann calls it the airplane of poetry, which you can hear buzzing high up in the sky on a summery day. People think she is actually interested in airplanes and give her books for her birthday which explain historically how man always wanted to be able to fly and now jets. Everywhere on the streets Ann sees utter strangers wearing shirts with an airplane design, often obvious biplanes, and airplanes exploited everywhere just the way mushrooms used to be. She lets the airplanes on her shelf gather dust. Ann gives up having fetishes and all of America moves into trailers.

Lost and Found

Mommy was sweeping the floor on which there was no dirt. Daddy was off in the world "looking for work." Ann was holding the dustpan for Mommy, and Ben was sitting in the corner, bored. Even though Ann and Ben were children, they knew there was no dirt on the floor. Ann felt sorry for Mommy. She thought she was a little crazy. But if she had to be a little crazy to get the floor clean Ann could allow for it. It was not the way she would have done it, but then, she was not Mommy. She knew that Ben didn't see it that way. She knew that Ben thought Mommy was trying to tell them something by the way she swept the floor.

Then Mommy spoke to them. She was leaning on her broom. "Take the basket of breadcrumbs," she said, "and go off into the forest and gather berries." "OK, Mommy," Ann said, jumping up without thinking. Ben got up slowly and looked at Ann as if to tell her something she already knew. But she didn't know what he was talking about. She picked up the basket and took Ben's arm and they walked into the forest. "Mommy's trying to get rid of us," Ben said. "She wants us to get lost in the forest." "Don't be silly," Ann said. "After all, she gave us these crumbs!" "Exactly," Ben said. "Anyway, what a pretty forest!" Ann said, skipping along. "Oh yeah, what a beautiful forest," Ben said. "It's full of monsters."

"I wonder where all the berries are," Ann said. "There aren't any berries," Ben said. "The monsters have eaten them all." "Well, let's have lunch, anyway," Ann said. They sat down and looked in the basket. "Breadcrumbs!" Ben said. "That's not enough to feed a bird!" He threw the breadcrumbs into a bush. Pretty soon, two birds came out and ate them. "You see, you were wrong, Ben," Ann said. "There's enough to feed two birds."

Ben looked at her in disgust. Ann looked at Ben and saw that he was brown as a berry. "Why are you staring at me like that?" Ben demanded. "I wasn't staring at you like anything," Ann said. "Would you like to play a staring game?" she asked. "Oh get lost!" Ben said.

Ann was lost. She was truly lost. She was so lost that Ben had to get lost to find her. "Now we're lost," Ben said. "And it's all your fault. You made us get lost on purpose." Ann started to cry. It was getting dark, and she was hungry. "Great," Ben said. "First you get us lost, then you have to cry to make things worse." "I'm sorry," Ann said. "It's all my fault. I promise not to interfere anymore."

They walked on for a while past all the places where Ann noticed that there had recently been berries and where Ben remarked that there had recently been monsters. "Look, there's a house!" Ann cried. "That's not a house, that's only made to look like a house," Ben said. "How do you know that?" Ann asked. "A little bird told me," Ben said. "Well, I don't care," Ann said. "I can smell something cooking!"

They went into the house. Mommy was getting ready to bake something in the oven. "Come in, children," Mommy said. "You're just in time. Wipe your feet." Ben pulled Ann aside. "Mommy's going to try to put me in her oven," he whispered to Ann. "Oh, Ben, don't be silly," Ann said.

Mommy gave Ben a little poke with her broom. "You're awfully thin, Ben," she said. "I'm going to have to fatten you up." "Oh, no you don't!" Ben cried, and he pushed her in the oven and shut the door. "Oh, God, what have I done?" he said. "Why did you let me do it, Ann?" Ben screamed. Ann sat down in the corner. Soon Daddy would be home. But what did that matter now?

"Hello children!" Daddy called from the doorway. "What's cooking?" "Oh Daddy," Ann blurted out. "It's Mommy!" "Yes," said Ben, "and now I will have to go to the gas chamber." "Well, let's not get hasty," Daddy said. "After all, Mommy was a wicked witch." "You see," Ann said. "Everything's going to be all right." "No, I don't see," Ben said. "Well, we'll talk about it at dinner," Daddy said, coming in and putting his basket of berries on the table. Ben watched him track dirt all across the floor. "I'm ready to go to the gas chamber," he repeated. But Daddy wasn't listening. "Daddy's a monster," Ben said to Ann. Ann started to set the table. "Well, if Daddy has to be a monster in order for there to be a happy ending, I think we should let him," she said.

Imitation of a Story

The mother cat imitated to the people of the house the ideal of motherhood. The two ducks imitated a happy couple, and thus set an example. The dog imitated loyalty and affection to the delight of the entire household. Ben imitated the breadwinner, and brought home imitation bread. At dinner, the child imitated a child and acted as if he weren't eating his vegetables. Ann imitated concentration while driving and thus was enabled to get home in time to fix dinner. After dinner, Ben imitated sincerity when he offered to do the dishes, and Ann imitated gratitude all the while thinking, "It's about time!" Ben wasn't able to finish the dishes, however, because just as he began the doorbell rang. They looked at each other and mirrored exasperation. Ann really was exasperated—she didn't want to see anyone just then. She was tired of imitating herself. She had done it all day in order to deal with other people. She had imitated somebody who possibly would buy the things in the store for the saleslady; she had imitated a woman who should be treated with quick, efficient and polite service at the gas station; she had imitated a person who really desired to work at her job interview. And the saleslady had pretended that she was dealing with a prospective buyer; the gas station attendant had acted the role of someone whose only dimension was his quick efficient service; and the man who had interviewed her for the job pretended that he sincerely did want to hire her, but there were others, higher up, which he could do nothing about, unhappily, who prevented such a privilege from being bestowed. Ann had wanted to believe the man, but it was just as well. She really didn't want to work. But now her conscience was clear. She had imitated all the steps a sincere person follows when he wants a job. And her husband was secretly glad when the doorbell rang. Actually, he didn't want to do the dishes, but wanted to seem to his wife like a fair and kindly husband. "Well, that's that," he said, taking off his rubber gloves which were not really made out of rubber. Ann looked angry, but already her face was changing. Now it looked hospitable. Ben went over to the door and opened it, but there wasn't anybody there. He was really astonished. "Wasn't that the doorbell?" he asked. Ann's face had changed again. Now it looked something like concern. Now it looked puzzled. It was trying not to look like fear. They both looked at the dog. They wanted him to act like he knew what was going on, to sniff around the door, or to bark or growl. He wagged his tail a little bit, but soon saw that this wasn't what the people wanted. So he looked sheepish. "I thought it was the doorbell," Ann said. "Perhaps there's a wire crossed somewhere or something." But the dragon, from the story the child was reading in his little bed upstairs, had the last word.

Sociology

He becomes taller, heavier, and stronger. He walks, he talks, he writes, he rides a bicycle. He has sex relations.

He has memorized the poem, and he has worked out his algebra problems. And now he can imagine love scenes!

"He" can be characterized as shy, modest, bold, persistent, frugal, and friendly. That is all very well. That sounds like information. But that still doesn't tell us what behavior to expect from a doctor or a department store clerk, what hardware stores or hos-pit-als are for, what utensils to use when eating specific foods, how to behave in church, or what to do when giving a party, now, does it? And *we* don't know what feelings he develops towards his sister, either. What standards of right and wrong *does* he uphold if he is inadvertently rude, or if he fails an examination?

He speaks English, but the next guy speaks only in Russian. He eats his rice with chop-sticks, but the man next to him is using his fork. The man next to him is standing and feeling proud when they play "La Marseillaise," but that means next to nothing to him. He is deeply respectful of his father, but the next guy refers to his father as a "pal" or "Dad." He it is who feels somber and serious at a funeral while the other guy is expressing strong emotion. (One might eat grasshoppers with relish while another turned away in disgust.)

Men wear trousers and shirts, and women—although less so today—wear dresses. Men shake hands when they are introduced to one another. "We" say "hello" when we answer the phone. "We" express sympathy when we meet someone who has just suffered some tragic loss. He not only knows what is expected of him and behaves accordingly, he also thinks that this is the proper way for him to think and behave!

In some groups, it is considered worthy to contribute to charity, to be loyal to one's friends, and to express feelings of patriotism, and it is considered wrong to snub old friends, marry for money, or to have an affair with someone else's wife.

The taxi driver has a right to ask you for your fare and the obligation to drive you to your destination; the doctor has a right to ask you about your symptoms and, in some instances, to have you remove your clothes—and he has the obligation to try to cure you.

A cat that toys with a mouse is unaware of the feelings of the mouse and therefore is not "cruel," nor is a large dog that attacks a small one and takes his bone "unkind." The need for food may be satisfied by eating meat, vegetables, or even people. The sex needs may be expressed directly, or, if not, they can always be sublimated in dancing, art, and religious ceremonies. Although no amount of training can enable a person to function in given ways before he is biologically ready.

He is the good soldier, he not only obeys his superior on the battlefield, he also feels that it is right and proper for the officer to issue the commands. He has learned the language, distinguished between the behavior of boys and girls, and attended school. Now he must himself decide what foods to eat, how to spend his money, and what girls to take out.

For certain behavior is expected of him, and others modify their behavior accordingly. He is expected to cry when he is uncomfortable, to sleep when he is sleepy, and to excrete without restraint. Since he is unfamiliar with the ways of society he depends upon others for care and for decisions concerning his welfare.

So, in the end, he gets strong biological enjoyment. He spends a great deal of his nights in sexual exploration. Recreation, relaxation, and pure laziness from Friday night through Sunday are extremely satisfying experiences. If such a weekend leaves the worker too exhausted to get on the job on Monday, he will be on the job by Tuesday. For only by seeing himself as an object can he know how to check, guide, and judge his own behavior, and act according to others' expectations.

Johnny Fuckfaster

One day Johnny Fuckfaster went over to visit his little friend Bobby. Bobby was only nine years old, but Johnny treated him like a grown-up. He often spirited him off to the wax museum and showed him the chamber of horrors, which was in the basement. Bobby's folks had, of course, forbidden him to go down in the basement, so Bobby didn't tell them. As Johnny always said, "What you don't know won't hurt you."

But today Bobby couldn't go, because he and his family were about to go to a party. Johnny hadn't been invited. It wasn't going to be that kind of a party, that's all. It wasn't that Bobby's family were ashamed of Johnny. Everyone in Bobby's family was fond of Johnny. He was good with Bobby, he was always cheerful, he played the piano, and he knew how to sing. Bobby's mother, it was true, didn't wholly approve of Johnny. She knew he was not quite nice. But that was really why she liked Johnny so much. And she knew that Johnny was good for Bobby. Bobby's father was fond of Johnny, too, although he pretended to disapprove of him.

Bobby's father was leaving for the party early. "I'll meet you over there later," he said to his family. "I'll see you later," he said to Johnny. Then he left. "Come on," Johnny said to Bobby's sister, Ann. "Let's play a game." "No," Ann said. "I have to get ready for the party now. I have to take a shower." Johnny and Bobby's sister Ann were always fighting. "Ok," said Johnny, looking down the hall to make sure there was nobody there. Then he followed Ann into the bathroom and locked the door. A minute later Johnny came out and found Bobby and asked him where they kept the towels. Bobby took him to a cupboard, but he didn't look him in the eye. He was all dressed up in his party clothes. He was very grown up.

Johnny took two towels from the cupboard. He looked down the hallway. There was nobody there. Then he went back in in the bathroom and locked the door. Ann was having trouble getting the shower to work. Johnny took off his clothes. Ann already had hers off. She was leaning over the tub, and Johnny came up behind her. She couldn't make the shower work. "You'll have to get down on the floor," Johnny said. Ann got down on her back on the floor. That was how she came to see the underside of the tub for the first time. "Oh, Johnny Fuckfaster!" she cried. She could hear her mother, her brother, and her grandfather walking up and down the hall outside.

In a little while, Johnny leaped up and went to the door. He called for Bobby. "Get the shower to work," he said to Bobby. Johnny had a towel wrapped around his middle. Ann peeked out at Bobby from behind the shower curtain. She smiled at Bobby. He didn't look her in the eye. He turned the shower on, and he left the room.

Johnny got in the shower with Ann. When he was dry, he peeked out the door to see if there was anybody there, waiting to use the bathroom. Then he went and hid in Bobby's room while they all left for the party. Ann had pleaded a stomach ache, and had been allowed to stay home. When they had all left, Ann and Johnny went and lay down in Bobby's room, where the t.v. was. For decency's sake, they got in the bed the wrong way, so their heads were at the foot of the bed. During the commercial, Johnny got up and raided the refrigerator. Then he got back in bed and spread a feast of toast and jam on Ann's chest, and leaned over her eating. Just then they heard a noise. "It's the dog," Ann said. Johnny hid under the covers. Then Ann's father walked in. Ann explained to Daddy that the others had already left for the party, and were expecting to meet him there. "What are you doing here?" Daddy asked. "I have a stomach ache," Ann said. "Well, I see you haven't lost your appetite," Daddy said. There was food all over the bed. "You've made a fine mess in here," Daddy said. "I don't know what Bobby will think."

Johnny had an uninteresting job down in the industrial section of town down by where the bay was polluted. One day, Bobby's sister Ann brought Johnny a picnic lunch there. They went out on the grass, but there were ants. "Follow me," Johnny said, Johnny always acted like he knew where he was going. They crawled through some barbed wire that said "Danger" and walked along a pier that said "Keep off." There was a boy fishing on the beach, but he was in the distance. Ann didn't know how well he could see. Johnny perched on a piling and took down his pants. Then he took Ann's pants down and perched her on him. "Oh, Johnny Fuckfaster!" she cried. The boy was approaching.

One day Johnny took Bobby and Ann over to Uncle Ed's to watch color t.v. Bobby was only nine years old and wanted to watch a kiddie program. Johnny was always nice to Bobby so he let him watch it. Then Johnny and Ann went into the other room in disgust. Uncle Ed was washing the dishes. "Let's go out on the porch," Johnny said to Ann. "But it's dark!" Ann protested. "Right," Johnny said, going out. "But it's raining," Ann said, following him. She had her rain boots on. Johnny unzipped his pants, and sat down on a little stool that was there. Light poured out from a window in the house. Ann took her pants part way down. But she couldn't get her leg over Johnny with her pants that way. She pulled one boot and one pant leg all the way off. Then Johnny pulled her down, so she was sitting on his lap, facing him. A car was coming down the road. "Oh, Johnny Fuckfaster," Ann cried softly. The car passed, and its headlights disappeared down the road. Ann and Johnny went back in the house. One of Ann's socks was wet.

"Your program is on now!" Bobby called from the other room. Ann and Johnny went in and sat in front of the t.v. Uncle Ed had finished washing the dishes. Ann took off her socks, and rolled up her jeans. Bobby was pretending he was a lion. He glared at Ann and Johnny, and showed them his claws. It was a good program.

Bobby was lying in bed reading an adventure story. The hero of the story was a little boy, nine years old. He and his sister were exploring a treasure island. They were looking for the treasure. They had a snack of toast and jam and then they went to look for the entrance to the cave. The boy's sister was always complaining. She was tired. She didn't want to go any further. Bobby's mother came in and told him to turn off the light and go to sleep. His mother left the room. The little boy said, "You wait here if you want to, Ann, I'm going to explore a bit further." Bobby heard a noise in the house. It was his father coming in. Bobby turned out his light, and pretended he was asleep. "OK," said Ann. "You go ahead. I can't go any further." The little boy set off alone down the passage. Soon, he was out of sight around a corner. Ann sat down on the cold floor and took off her boots. After a while, she heard some footsteps coming down the tunnel. "It must be Bobby," she thought. "I wonder if he has found the treasure." "Hello, Ann," said a voice. It was Bobby's friend, Johnny Fuckfaster. Ann took off her pants.

Letting the Music Stop
(As Told by Ann)

As Clarence entered the room he smelled the potato chips at once and knew at a glance exactly how many people were present. He saw each of us sitting, standing, slouching, and bending. He saw us, each face signaling out from among the others. He saw Prudence. Information relating to Prudence's person was effortlessly registered. Without strain Clarence would later be able to remember whether she had been wearing a dress, a pair of pants, or nothing. He would be able to accurately describe the material it was made of, the shape of her hips, the width of her belt, or the disposition of the areolae round each nipple. He could recreate her position in the room just as it was when he came in. And he could describe where each of us had been standing as well as what was on the mantel and exactly what that was on the rug. He had seen at a glance where the silk lay and where the wool!

Prudence was watching as Clarence appeared in the doorway. She noted the way he came in, his hair, and the expression on his face. She noted his clothes and she noted the way he walked. All this made a deep impression on her, although you wouldn't know that to look at her face, which was absolutely blank. No wonder we think she is dull and stupid! She just stands there, and you can't tell what's going on. It doesn't look like anything's going on. In fact, she looks like a block of wood. Anyway, the first thing Clarence did when he came in was to tell one of his long involved jokes. But did Prudence laugh? Of course not. She looked as blank as ever. But that was only because she didn't get it.

It was quiet for a while, and then Enzo, with his eyes half-shut, told us what the weather would be tomorrow. His prediction turned out to be amazingly accurate, as usual. Which is odd when you consider what a mess of a person Enzo is. I mean, half the time he doesn't even know what he's doing. I mean he's always late and he'd forget his head if it weren't attached to his neck. The next thing you know Enzo had fainted, and everyone jumped up, surprised. But what can you expect from a person who forgets to eat and sleep? Clarence, of course, noticed right away that Enzo had fainted, and Pru, naturally, noticed the manner of his fainting. Then Clarence started to freak out. He was suddenly convinced that Enzo had brought a horrible contagious disease into the room and that he was going to catch it and die. Clarence was afraid when he thought of losing all his money, also.

Fortunately, Ten-sing was there. He's always eager to put order back into any situation. "Wait a minute," Ten-sing said, coming forward to where Enzo lay stretched across the floor. "One should first get to the basic facts and then see how to proceed."

This made Hortense look up from the huge bowl of potato chips she had just finished without realizing it. She was surprised to see Enzo lying there—she had had no idea, and how long had he been like that? She made a prophecy. Then she went into the bathroom. A quarter of an hour later she came out and said to Clarence, "You know, I've been in the bathroom fifteen minutes and I just noticed that there are vines growing all over it." "You're kidding," he said, "I noticed that the moment I went in there." "What kind of vine was it, Hortense?" Ten-sing was moved to ask. "Oh, I dunno—ivy? Doesn't ivy make vines? Does anything else—are there other kinds of vines?" Hortense was impatient. She didn't see the importance of this conversation. Clarence was still disdainful of her for not noticing the vines in the first place. Ten-sing thought everyone was getting along splendidly—it was a party, after all, where people are supposed to have fun, so he assumed that we were. There is a right way and a wrong way to do things. And of course one would naturally choose the right way. And that is all there is to it. I just looked at Hortense and wondered what she had been doing in the bathroom for so long, and my judgement of who she is shifted slightly, again.

Clarence was explaining to us what kind of vine grew in the bathroom, what other types might have grown, and what types would never grow there in a million years, as any idiot knows. "You patronizing bastard," I thought. Then Prudence started laughing. She had just gotten Clarence's joke. Clarence, mistaking her amusement, bridled. "I'm sorry," he said, "I thought you wanted to know about these vines." But Prudence had been to the bathroom already. She had a clear inner picture of the vines.

All this time Florence had been looking after Enzo. She had gotten him up off the floor and onto the couch. She had loosened his collar and gotten him to eat something, and mopped his brow with a cool wash cloth. She was leaning over him and asking him how he felt, and what she could do for him, and telling him she was sure everything would be all right. "Never mind, Enzo, " she said. "It's still awfully good to see you after so long, isn't this a wonderful party, the weather today was so perfect!" But Florence's escort, Ten-sing, was impatient to leave. He couldn't understand why Florence was keeping him waiting. He was tugging on her sleeve. "Come on, already, let's go, Flo," he barked. "Just a minute, darling," Florence said. She just wanted to get Enzo a glass of water. And she had to thank her hostess and of course have a final drink with everyone. Anyway, where was her purse? "I'll wait in the car," Ten-sing said, reasonably enough. "Oh, go fuck yourself," she screamed, suddenly throwing a block of ice at him. Who would have guessed that Florence could ever be so cold and unaccommodating? Not that Ten-sing seemed to mind. He wasn't fazed a bit. For the truth is, he loves Florence as well, as sincerely, and as devotedly as her large dog loves her.

Enzo was watching to see what would develop. For Enzo saw what was not yet visible—the future, possible and potential in the background of the situation.

I, also, was thinking towards the future—the near future, hopefully, when everyone would leave. I had come to the decision that the party had ended quite a while ago, although no one had gone home, except, perhaps, for myself, who had been home all along, although it was hardly home anymore with all these strange types invading it. I couldn't understand why I had had the party in the first place. "Come back," said Enoch, always thoughtful, "to basic concepts and ask yourself what you are really doing mentally." "What?" I said. "What right," he said, "does one have to judge this party? First we should understand what we mean by party. Par-ty. Otherwise we shall get into a muddle. Mud-dle." I had no rejoinder to this. STILL WATERS RUN DEEP. Later I asked Pru how I could get everyone to go, and she said "Let the music stop," and I did.

FROM THE WINDOW

A Dress's Truth

I am a dress, hanging on a hanger, hanging on the rack towards which Ann is approaching. I saw her walk into the store, hoping not to be noticed. She must hope that she looks casual. Some of the other "things" on the rack start to scream and shout. She is scrutinizing and scanning all of us things like a teller counting money—it isn't hers, but perhaps some of it could be!

Perhaps I am the dress that can reveal her true beauty! The dress that could go anywhere, which brings warmth in the winter and refreshment in summer! Perhaps I am the dress which befriends her till death! Perhaps not. She reaches towards me, and then her arm goes slack.

I hang in my folds, bodiless. There are so many of us things all around that she can't be sure I stand out. She reaches out and touches my material.

Frankly, it's possible that I'm trying to fool her, and am actually quite ugly. Or I might be too expensive, or too cheap, too shoddy. One moment she is reading my tag in a neutral tone and the next she has me in the dressing room and is ripping me from the hanger.

Her old clothes twist on the floor. I am on top of her; she

is inside of me. We move back and forth in the mirror. This is either some avant garde style, or it's something pretty dumb. She turns from side to side, trying for a glimpse of the truth.

A Man and His Dog

Once there was a man who was very proud of his dog. He was very proud one day when the dog chewed up one of the boots which the man had left outside his front door. He was proud that the dog had taken not only that boot but its mate out to the place in the field where he waited for his master to return. Then both would go inside and sit by the fire until bedtime. At which point the dog would be put out.

And so his dog ran free all the night long and all the day, and people in the neighborhood came to call him by different names—Grey-muzzle, and Charcoal—and they would pretend he was their dog. But when the time drew near for the man to return, the dog would leave whatever he was doing and go to his place in the field to wait for him.

But one day when the man came home the dog wasn't there, waiting. After a while the man started to worry and to feel sorry that he had once thrown one of his boots at the dog. Then the man thought to call the pound. Sure enough, his dog was down there. He was behind bars. So the man had to bail him out.

Now this man wasn't made of money. So he decided to fence his yard so the dog wouldn't be picked up anymore.

In the meantime, the dog was brought in the house. Now he had to be walked and exercised every day. Now the dog had to be led by a chain past all the other dogs in the neighborhood. He was no longer allowed out without supervision. The man was very busy, and didn't have time to fence his yard.

Years passed, and the dog grew sleepy. His hair started to fall out, and the rug floated with dog fur. After a while, he stopped going to the door to ask to be let out. His energy flagged, and his eyes glazed over. He had lost interest in just about everything but fleas.

As for the man, the sight of his own dog had become abhorrent to him. At first he felt bad, until one day it came to him as a shocking revelation—he had never really loved his dog in the first place.

Nobody's Business

Since Pam had business in Dick's part of the state it was natural that she should stay at his place. When Pam's husband Sam had had business in Dick's part of the state, he had stayed with Dick, and when Dick had business in Pam and Sam's part of the state he had stayed with them. They all liked to have business in each other's parts of the state.

So one day when Dick was visiting in Pam and Sam's part of the state Pam told Dick that she had business soon in his part of the state, and Dick said, "Well, then, you must come and stay with me," and Pam said, "Thanks, I was counting on it," and Sam said, "I don't care *what* you two get up to together, Dick, as long as you don't take her away from me," and everybody laughed.

When Pam got off the plane in Dick's part of the state Dick was there to meet her just as he had been when Sam had come down. They greeted each other with a big hug the way friends do just to show one another how much they like each other.

On the way back in the car they talked about Dick's love-life. Dick claimed to be having trouble with his love-life and Pam claimed disbelief. She didn't see how anyone as handsome and charming and intelligent as Dick could be having any trouble with his love-life. And Pam knew that Dick made a point of not being a male chauvinist. So she was surprised when Dick insisted she sleep in his bed while he camped on the couch. Dick insisted—he liked to give his friends the pleasure of sleeping in his bedroom. His bedroom was very special, with a window opening on the sea.

Pam had brought her negligée, since she thought it would be hot down there. She put it on, and went downstairs to brush her teeth. It was a rose colored nightgown which she didn't wear very often at home, because it was too cold. It had a robe of flowing midnight blue which revealed a little of the pink nightgown at the hem which Dick noticed when he was bedding down for the night. Pam didn't take the robe off when she went upstairs and crawled into bed. It was a little wrinkled when she came downstairs to use the bathroom in the morning. Dick was already up and was standing in the kitchen frying some eggs for her.

"Good morning!" Pam said brightly, going into the bathroom. It was a small house, and the bathroom was conveniently right off the kitchen. Pam sat down on the toilet and started to pee.

"I wonder if part of the problem I'm having with women lately has to do with that bathroom," Dick said. "What do you mean?" Pam said, peeing. "Sometimes I think women are embarrassed to piss here. This place is so small you can hear it from the living room." "It's a good thing I don't have any inhibitions," Pam said, gayly flushing.

After breakfast Pam had a swim in Dick's pool. Sam had swum in Dick's pool when he was here and had told her how good it was. When she came in from the pool she said, "I feel just like Esther Williams." "You *look* just like Esther Williams," Dick said, politely.

That night at dinner Dick confessed to Pam that he wondered if part of the problem he was having with his love-life lately wasn't that he was watching the relationship too closely as it unveiled. Pam assured him that his qualms were only illusory. That night she slept in her robe again.

The next day they told each other what a good time they were having with each other, and wasn't it great when men and women could be chums, and Dick said, "I hope Sam doesn't really think that anything's going on between us," and Pam said, "Oh, no, that was only a joke!"

Now they had only a little time left together, and an evil gleam came into Dick's eye, and he said, "Why don't we go out and get some doughnuts?" "Yes, let's go!" Pam said daringly, and they looked at each other like conspirators. At the doughnut shop Dick was just getting his money out to pay when Pam pushed his hand away. "Oh, no," Pam said. "You've got to let me pay for this." "No, I insist," Dick said. "Stop!" Pam said, throwing down her money. "You're treating me like a woman!"

Eating Cake

The first time Midge offered Emily a piece of cake she refused. Midge was the woman who had been married to the man Emily was involved with. She was being polite, but Emily knew cake was poison.

The second time Midge offered her a piece of cake it was clear that she was treating Emily like any of her other guests. The cake looked good, but Emily refused because eating cake is bad for your health.

The third time she offered Emily a piece of cake she seemed to have forgotten that she had just offered it to her twice. It was as if she had never refused. "All right, I'll take some," Emily said.

But she regretted having given in. However, Midge didn't bring her any cake.

The fourth time Midge offered Emily a piece of cake was just as she was leaving. "No thanks," she said. They were being civilized about the whole thing.

The Way Out

Nina was walking her neighbor, Rick Archer, through the back room to the door. They were talking about pussycats. Rick put his hand on the knob and stood there looking at it. Nina saw that Rick was having trouble getting out the door, so she made another little remark about pussycats. Rick twisted the doorknob and looked Nina full in the face. "He's going to tell me something," Nina thought. She quickly made a remark about pussycats. "There's something I have to tell you," Rick said.

"Well, I don't know *that* much about pussycats, but—" Nina began.

"I'm sexually attracted to you," Rick said.

Nina stared down at the kitty litter.

"But you're my neighbor's wife," he concluded, and he opened the door.

He was standing on the threshold. Nina was on the spot.

"I'm glad you feel that way," she said.

Rick stepped forward and gave Nina a hug. Nina gave it back to him. Now he could go.

The Lost Key

He sat at the bar sipping his drink. He might have come there with companions, for all *they* knew! *He* knew he had come there by himself. Wasn't it obvious? He was available, or rather, he glanced around to see who else there might be available. Next to him at the bar sat his liver and his pancreas. They were discussing him. Let them! It was no concern of his. If they wanted to do him harm, that was their business. *He* certainly didn't wish anybody any harm. They might talk about him all they pleased, but they would never get inside him, really know him. Even if he managed to get them to come home with him for the night they would only accompany the image of himself. The image of himself might do one thing or another, and this would provide some amusement for him, who was there also, watching.

No, they would never get inside him because he was all locked up, and had taken the precaution of throwing away the key. He ordered another drink. Having another drink wouldn't harm anybody, only himself. It wasn't harming them. They might be speculating about what drove him to drink. What a noise they made! He had another. Why sip, he realized, and wouldn't it be grand if he could only slip off the bar stool which was so uncomfortably high and slide down on the floor? Then they would probably rush over and offer to pick him up. Then he would ask them to come home with him. They would ask him what he was doing on the floor. They would assume that he was out of his senses. That he was drunk. That's all *they* knew! But he would tell them, tell them that he had a perfectly good reason for crawling about on the floor. He had lost something. (They could go through the pretense of helping him look for it if they wished, if that was their idea of foreplay. But he would get them to drive him home in the end.) He had lost his key!

Heat, The Victim of Light

When he did most of the cooking, she did most of the cleaning up. That was only fair. Vacuuming was a fair exchange for laundry. Neither wanted to go shopping, so both went, in order to be fair. It was not fair to make him worry, so when she stayed away she let him know not to expect her ahead of time. It was not fair to expect her to stay home every night, so he never did. If he cooked a special little tidbit for her, however, it was only fair of her to eat it. If he wanted to sleep alone some nights, then she wanted to sleep alone some nights. Neither took unfair advantage of the other. They held each other in mutual respect, and sometimes, when she held him to her in the night she wondered if this wasn't love, after all. But by day it was clear, it was only fair.

Outside of Tradition

Ken was born into a traditional Jewish community in Toronto. Everything was fine until his father died. He rode his little car down the sidewalk. How could he be a man for his mother and sister?

His mother moved them to Los Angeles where she thought an uncle would help them. He didn't. In Los Angeles there was no sense of tradition or responsibility. So his mother married a man, Morrie, who she thought would give her financial security. Morrie could not replace her dead husband. They fought. The children grew up. Ken wanted to get away. He went to college as far away as he could get.

He fell in love with a woman. He was still a virgin. It was his first love. But she was married. The woman was unlike anyone else to him. She was a mother.

She had two children, but not by her present husband. She had only married him for financial security. Ken often visited at her house and the husband was none the wiser, the woman was so much older than Ken. The husband often fixed Ken's car.

Ken longed for the day when the woman would leave her husband and live with him. She couldn't leave him for a while—not until she was through law school—since he was putting her through. Ken couldn't offer her any financial security—he was just a boy—hardly grown up. So sometimes while the husband was out in the garage fixing the car which he had arranged for Ken to buy originally anyway, if the kids were sleeping or out back, then Ken and the woman would go at it quietly in the spare room of the tract house with the blinds pulled down.

Needless so say, after the woman passed the bar examination and indeed left her husband, she didn't go live with Ken as he had assumed she would. She said she didn't like the way he left his clothes lying on the floor.

Where There's Smoke

Nan's husband wanted to stop smoking so people would stop trying to make him feel bad that he smoked. And so he stopped smoking. "How long has it been since you stopped smoking?" his family and friends would ask him, and he would add up the figures with the fluttery fingers of one hand. The other was behind his back with its fingers crossed, for he was still smoking secretly.

Yet for the time he still spent with his family and friends he was truthfully not smoking. He was so convincing as a non-smoker that he thought to himself, "There's nothing to it, really!" His real goal, however, was not so much to stop as to cut down. And wasn't this being accomplished by only being able to smoke out here on the driveway while his friends in the house sat thinking he was going to the bathroom? He was getting tired of these people and their sanctimony. His burning butt fell to the concrete and he squashed it.

Back in the house, now, they asked him "How long?" How long had it been since he'd quit? He would show them. He raised his right hand, moving the fingers as those of the other hand moved under the table, under the skirt of a certain young lady. His wife would probably say he was cheating on her if she knew. But she didn't know, so who was he cheating?

A Freak Appearance

Ann always said she liked freaks. She was, she said, one of them, in the sense that we all are secretly mad. So Ann didn't panic standing naked in the shower one day at the "Y" after swimming when she was entirely surrounded by female freaks—classically sweet pinheads, hydrocephalics, and other phenomena bubbling and crawling on the floor. One touched her. Ann hoped her recoil didn't hurt anyone's feelings and would stave off further attacks. These were simply naked female bodies. What did make Ann stand out?

Ann dried herself and dressed at her locker, going quickly through motions which took longer than she remembered while the freaks sat on benches holding pieces of underwear with puzzled expressions. A girl was trying to strap her bra to her knee. "That could be me," Ann thought.

Without looking anyone in particular in the eye, Ann made it to the door and to the lobby. Her friend wasn't out yet. Ann glanced through the big double glass window threaded with wire into the pool. It was empty except for one freak at this end in a white swimcap.

It smiled at Ann. Ann watched it float back and forth before her. Then it shoved some water towards Ann which slopped on the window. Ann stepped back a bit. Perhaps she *had* been staring. The freak started to wave at her. "Why is she waving at me?" Ann thought, without waving back. The freak was waving more and more violently. Ann didn't wave back. She wasn't going to be tricked by this freak into playing along with its game. What did it know? What did it think she was?

It rose from the pool and strode towards the dressing room removing its cap. Then Ann saw that it was no more a freak than she was. It was her friend Sherril, and she looked mad!

The World of Consequences

Molly Shapiro was a junior in college. Her boyfriend had just dumped her, but she wasn't down in the dumps. On the contrary, she was spending every evening in the neighboring apartment, talking and joking with the two young men who shared it—Ricky Polstein and John O'Hare. Molly enjoyed both of them, but she had a crush on John, who had a fierce black moustache. No wonder John ended up spending the night in her bed!

However, this evening was more innocent than it might sound, for once under the covers they each discovered that the other didn't have any birth control. So what could they do, being intelligent college juniors? Nothing.

Shortly after that, Molly started going out with one of her professors who, being an intelligent college professor, sent her to get birth control pills.

This professor's name was Dan Smith, and though he was several years older than Ricky and John, he became friendly with them, also, and when John eventually married a rather plain though very perky young woman named Joan and when Molly became Mrs. Dan Smith the professor's wife they all were still friends even though Molly and Dan moved one place and John and Joan another and Ricky practically disappeared.

Many years went by, and Molly discovered that being a college professor's wife was not quite what she had imagined it would be. Dan had many affairs with his students, and Molly was always learning about them just as they were ending. Finally, Molly discovered one that had gone on for nine months with a woman named Lenore. Molly was just about devastated, although Dan assured her that it was all over and, of course, would never happen again. He thought, moreover, that Molly should have some pity for Lenore, and related her story.

Lenore had been married to a musician. She thought she was happily married even though she was frigid, and one night she finally did have an orgasm. She thought that her troubles were over, but just then her musician husband confessed to her that he was having an affair. Lenore had never had another orgasm after that, and shortly thereafter they were divorced and Lenore appeared in one of Dan's classes.

When Molly heard this story she wished that she herself was frigid since Dan found that so attractive, but she also cursed Lenore for thinking that she could revenge herself on her ex-husband by doing to Molly what had been done to her.

Molly was still trying to reconcile all her feelings when suddenly John O'Hare appeared on her doorstep. He was passing through on his way south. Joan had not been able to accompany him on this trip. He wondered if he might spend the night on their couch.

Molly was very glad to see him. Unfortunately, she told him, Dan had a night class and wouldn't be home until late.

John said he was sorry, but he did not look sorry. He leaned back in his seat so that the sun caught the aquamarine dazzle of his eyes. Then Molly knew that they were finally going to make love after all these years. After all the affairs Dan had had she couldn't see any reason why she shouldn't have this one moment with John. It seemed like a godsend, for she thought it might help her to stop hating Dan so much. If she did it too, then the score would be even.

However, when Dan found out, he was, to Molly's surprise, very angry, and it wasn't many more years before they were divorced.

During that time she never heard from John and Joan and surmised that John had told Joan and that she now hated Molly. Molly was sorry, for she had treasured their friendship. But she always asked mutual friends for news of them, and one day when Ricky Polstein was in town she heard from him that Joan had become very promiscuous, and had had to have a series of abortions because of her many affairs. In fact, there had been five such abortions. Five little graves with five little headstones were erected to them. And that is why when Molly died and was brought before the Judge she was accused of having murdered five babies in the world of consequences.

On the Horns of Plenty

The wedding was taking place in an elegant rented hall in the middle of a wild wood, in the conscious mind surrounded on all sides by the unconscious. As Ann tripped in through the French doors she realized that she didn't recognize a soul.

Although actually everyone looked just like the bride and room. Everyone but Ann. What had possessed her to get all dressed up and come all the way out here? She barely knew the bride and groom. "You have to be there," they had said. "We're writing our own wedding ceremony." It was a social obligation. She thought she would just put her present down on the table by the horns of plenty and leave.

But a voice was calling, "Everybody stand in a circle!" "The circle of friendship," Ann thought. "The continuous circle of life." "Stand in the circle!" the voice said. Ann couldn't very well refuse. She could leave right after the ceremony. She came forward and stood almost in the circle. Okay, she would stand in the circle. But if they asked her to hold hands she was going to refuse. Then the voice asked her to hold hands and hands held hers. "The hands of supplication. The hands of communion," Ann thought. They were clammy hands.

The voice was coming from a man standing with arms

upraised in front of a huge stone fireplace. "The hearth of the home. The hearth of creation," Ann thought. There was a huge fire blazing in the fireplace. "The fire of desire. The undying flame of love. The Heraklitean flux. The fire which purifies all." Ann realized that he must be the minister. Ann was starting to sweat. It was a hot day.

Clasping the minister's hand in the air was the hand of the woman standing next to him. Ann realized that she must be the minister's wife. The archetypal couple. Adam and Eve. Mother and Father. Cupid and Psyche. Tarzan and Jane, mirroring the bride and groom, who were standing opposite them in the circle dressed as Faust and Marguerite.

The minister was talking about God, and what He had done to make this possible. The minister's wife was talking about God, and what She had done to make this possible.

Then the groom burst into a Hebrew chant, and everyone was very silent. He then did a few Indian chants, both American and East, and something Japanese. "All creatures are as one. The one in the many. Variety is the spice of life." Then the bride began to recite passages from great literature. In all these passages marriage was somewhere mentioned. Then Ann noticed that she didn't have it by heart. She was reading from a script. Everyone else seemed to be holding a script also.

"I now enjoin you to all join in responsive reading," the minister read. "I am you and you are me," the groom read. "I am you and you are me," everybody repeated. "You are me and I am you," the bride said. "You are me and I am you," everybody repeated. "They are us and we are them," the woman next to the groom read. "They are us and we are them," everybody repeated. "We are them and they are us," the man next to the bride said, and everybody said that we were them and they were us. "I am one and you are one," the man next to the woman next to the groom was saying when Ann realized that soon it would be her turn. She might have to sit down.

But before Ann could sit down the minister enjoined them to join in silent prayer. "The power of meditation. The pregnant silence. The silence that throws speech into relief." While it was silent Ann glanced around the circle. Everyone was either looking down at their shoes or looking upwards towards heaven with eyes closed. Everyone but the woman with the movie camera and the man extending a microphone on a boom. "Oh stop, thou art so fair. This wedding will last forever," Ann thought.

But the trance was broken when the minister enjoined the bride and groom to come forward and say their vows. And so they promised to love each other by honoring themselves, and that obedience had nothing to do with it, for as long as they did. Then they put their rings on their own fingers. "Self-determination. Double self-determination," Ann saw. And as they kissed the camera raised to catch the raising of a handkerchief to a pair of eyes on the other side of the circle.

Then, before anyone could leave the circle, a harlequin stepped forward with a guitar and explained that everyone was to join in on the verse. "The wisdom of fools. The universal language of music." He sang and played until everyone joined in on the verse, verse after verse, until no one know when to stop. "Song without end," Ann sang along. But then finally the minister said "Everyone mill around now. Mill! Mill!" But the bride and groom started going around the circle hugging everyone and the bride was at the woman next to Ann, hugging her and saying "I'm so glad that you're here!" And then the bride was at Ann, hugging her and saying "I'm so glad that you're here!" Ann hugged her back. The bride felt surprisingly small and insubstantial in her arms. Ann felt bad that she was here under false pretenses. Here was, after all, a little person just like herself.

When Ann was released she went to get a glass of champagne. She was going to have just one for the road. But while she was drinking a woman started talking to her. A woman who was also there alone. "What did you think of the ceremony?" she asked. "It really meant a lot to me," Ann said. Then she started to tell Ann about herself. She was a happily married woman. But she was having an affair. Her husband was upset, but he wouldn't admit it. Her husband would be here any minute. And she would like Ann to meet him, if it was all the same to her.

Decaying Flesh

Sometimes when she walks down her street she has to avert her eyes when she sees old people coming towards her walking their dogs. In the winter the dogs are wearing thin threadbare sweaters, though this is hardly enough to warm them, they are so old. What is terrible to see is a dog limping along in a sweater that has lost its shape, with its tail, which it only holds aloft with effort, sticking up. The terrible thing is this tail with the fur all rubbed off. God, don't let this happen to me! Sometimes the old people are just standing there on the sidewalk waiting for their dogs who are waiting for them, their fur gone from their bodies, their eyes glassing over. She looks down, and the other way, and meanwhile, inside the apartments where the old people live with their dogs, dry fur falls to the floor. The paint is hanging from the ceiling and coming off in great layers from the walls.

Enough to Handle

"See you later, dear," Marc called to Marlene as he made his way towards the door. "Daddy, wait, I'll open the door for you," Judy, who was five, called. "Goodby," Marc called to three year old Nelly. She raced to hug him around the legs. "It takes too long to get out of here," he said. Marlene looked up at the clock. It was 6:15. She was doing the dinner dishes. "When will you be home?" she asked Marc. Marc was working three nights a week now. "Daddy tell me a story tonight," Nelly said. "Daddy has to work. Mommy will tell you a story," Marlene said. "Mommy will tell you a story," Marc said. "Let me go, girls."

As soon as he was gone Marlene put Judy in the bath. Nelly was sitting on her bed "reading." Marlene dragged the exercycle into the foyer just outside the girls' bathroom and started to ride. She had turned forty and had decided that it was long past time for her to start taking care of herself. Halfway through her ride she jumped off and shampooed Judy's hair. Nelly started riding her tricycle into the exercycle. "Get away," Marlene said. She couldn't exercise as long as she wished. Judy wanted to get out of the bath. No, Judy didn't want to get out of the bath. Nelly wanted to get in with her.

Marlene took Judy out and put Nelly in. She wanted to take a shower herself. She took Nelly out and put both girls at the kitchen table with some pudding. They spilled the pudding on their stomachs. They laughed. Marlene wanted to take a shower.

"Do you want to go to bed right now, or do you want to play for half an hour?" Marlene asked. It was a mean question. Their bedtime was not for another half hour. Marlene wanted to take a shower before they went to bed. She didn't like taking a shower too late and going to bed with a wet head. She got in the shower. She could hear them screaming and noticed that she was not paying any attention. "Stop fighting or or or," she yelled. Judy came running in. "Molly's scratching me!" "What did you do to her?" Marlene just wanted to finish her shower. The phone rang. Marlene wondered if she was going to be electrocuted as she answered it. It was the mother of a girl Judy had become friendly with at school. Marlene could hear a baby screaming in the background.

Marlene arranged for the two girls to get together but she knew she would have to rearrange it later. Marlene was angry. "Come in and brush your teeth and go pee!" she yelled and yelled and yelled. The girls giggled and ran circles around her. Judy ran into the bathroom. Marlene came in. "Did you brush your teeth?" Judy was behind the door. There was a terrible noise. The towel bar had come loose and was now on the floor. Marlene examined it. She wondered if she would be able to plaster it back on. She had not gotten around to painting the furniture she had planned to paint last summer. She had turned forty and it was time she got around to something. But not this, not this. She didn't want this to happen. This was the kind of thing that she would never be able to get around to fixing. She pulled Judy out of the bathroom yelling at her like the ugly wicked witch that she was. Judy ran to her bed and cried and cried until Marlene told her that it was only a thing, the important thing was that no one was hurt. Nelly was whimpering that she was afraid of a witch. The ugly witch sat down and started to tell a story. They told her that the story wasn't long enough and wasn't interesting. She made it more interesting and longer, but she wasn't happy.

But Judy went to sleep. Nelly, however, did not, and was still awake when Marc came home at 9:30. She just wanted to give him a goodnight kiss.

The next day when Marlene woke up she had breast cancer. She was going to have to have radiation therapy. The news was very upsetting to her parents. Her parents were millionaires. They were almost afraid to ask her about it, but how was she going to pay for it? Did she have medical coverage?

She knew they didn't trust that she would have taken care of it. She asked Marc if he had sent in the forms. No, but he knew where they were. They were still covered until the end of the month! He wrote out a check and gave her the form to complete.

She had to put in the girls' birthdates. He didn't know the girls' birthdates. He had left out his social security number. She didn't know his social security number. She put the form with a check in an envelope and addressed it. Then she put a stamp on it and mailed it that very day.

Us

The ones in the very foreground look healthy but insignificant. They are reaching up from way down below. The ones behind them are taller with more tone, but they have seen too much sun. To the right it is sturdy, though small and prickly. Suddenly is a deep space to fall into between them and the middle distance, farther back and lower down. But they are followed by still another layer, now almost entirely in shadow. And still there is the background to contend with, now in sun and now in shade receding backwards into final definition against what is merely a shape not much denser than the sky.

The Realization of a Chicken

Once there was a chicken who was getting close to the end of her productivity. I am referring to her egg-laying ability, of course. Each chicken has only so many eggs backed up inside of it, and when a chicken hits forty it suddenly realizes what you might assume it knew all along—that its eggs are numbered.

I was wrong to say she was getting close to the end of her productivity. There was no reason why, even after her last egg had rolled away, all rotten and stinking to high heaven, there was no reason why she couldn't continue to be productive. Laying eggs wasn't the only thing a life was good for. Once she had been a young chick and hadn't laid any eggs, yet then she had never doubted that her life was worthwhile. But then, perhaps all along, in the back of her mind, the justification for her life had been based on her egg laying potential.

Actually, she wasn't going to miss egg laying when it stopped, she was sure. She wasn't going to miss the ups and downs of emotion or the mess and inconvenience. But it made her sad to think that she would never hatch any more eggs. She had only hatched two in all her life.

She had always wanted chicks, but the rooster who used to be in this barnyard had a violent temper and she didn't feel the chicks would be safe if she hatched any of the eggs which he had fertilized. He had strutted across the barnyard pecking randomly at whoever came in his way. She had been very relieved when he had been removed from the barnyard, though she cringed to think that he may have been made into rooster soup.

Miraculously, a new rooster was introduced into the barnyard who was a perfect match for her. This happened right before she became too old for this sort of thing. They quickly hatched two eggs together.

They had two adorable chicks, one after another, and for the next few years nobody got a complete night's rest. The chicks—one or the other or both—would wake up squawking, and then our chicken would have to get up off her roost and put them to sleep. But she waited so long to have chicks, that is, she had been deprived of them for so long that she never complained. However, she soon ran to fat and her thinking got fuzzy. Sometimes during this time she thought about hatching just one more chick, and she talked it over with the rooster who was neither for nor against the idea, and they talked it over for several years and then one day the chicken woke up and realized that it was too late. She was just too afraid of hatching a rotten egg now.

After all, weren't her two chicks enough? They ran her ragged, even though there were just two of them. But they were growing up. One day they were going to fly the coop. Then what would she do? A chicken, you must understand, can't simply go out and get a kitten.

And of course, the chicks did grow up and go away. We won't speculate on where they went. Our chicken was thrown back on her own devices. Gradually she started doing the things she used to do before she had had the chicks—she scratched for bugs, she crossed the road, etc. Gradually it dawned on her that she was her own person, so to speak; she was just herself, out in the world, and the world was simply there all around her. This was true for her and for all the other chickens equally. She and they were all simply there.

The Lonely Animal

Lately, when she had locked her door and was walking to the elevator, or, when she was coming down the hall after entering her apartment, she noticed the mewling of a cat. She had a cat, and for a while she assumed it was him, although it was a sound she had never heard him make. However, when she continued to her apartment she would find her own cat asleep on the top bunk in her girls' room, and, when she backtracked from the elevator and put her ear to her own door she heard nothing. The mewling wasn't coming from there. It was coming from the apartment next door.

She happened to know that two very nice cats lived in married bliss in that apartment. They had had an adorable litter of kittens and she herself had helped to place one in a good home. She wondered why they—or at least one of them—had started mewling. They never used to.

Then one day she met her neighbor at the elevator. He told her he was leaving for another state to go to court to try to get custody of his daughter from his ex-wife. She wished him luck and asked him if he would like her to feed his cats while he was gone.

Then he told her he had just one cat now. The male had

died of a mysterious disease of the nervous system just after his ex-wife had come to take his daughter, who had run away to live with him, away.

"I got her after I had him, so she doesn't know how to be alone," he said. "So she cries."

Ann thought of her own cat who had never lived with another and didn't seem to care.

Of course, when she had gotten guinea pigs for her daughters she had gotten two. There was something horrible about one guinea pig alone in a cage with nothing to do. She had visited at a house once where the people had one guinea pig in a glass tank and it had frightened her.

She thought of what a woman had told her yesterday. The woman had been married for twenty-five years although she hated her husband. She wanted to leave him, but she was afraid. She was afraid she'd be lonely.

The Whistling Man

There was a man who never spoke to her who lived on the ground floor of her building. He lived alone with two large old boxer dogs. She could tell they were old because they walked very slowly and their sweaters were very worn. She often passed the man with his boxers walking very slowly down the street or very slowly back to the building.

Rumor had it that this man had once been married and that his wife had left him. And that was why he never said hello to anybody coming in or going out. He had never recovered. He walked with his eyes lowered and his jowls drooping.

One day she saw the man who lived on the ground floor walking on crutches. The story got around that he had heard a noise in his apartment and had jumped out the window in terror, breaking his leg.

However, after a number of months, he appeared to have healed, and stopped appearing on his crutch, hobbling out to walk his dogs in the rain.

She didn't notice exactly when it happened, but one day she realized that one of the dogs had disappeared. The man was only walking one dog now, though the dog hardly could walk, but just hobbled along.

Then one day when she got in the elevator, instead of going directly up to her floor, it went down to the basement, where he entered. He must have been doing his laundry. He smelled like clean clothes. He didn't say hello. He stood with his back to her as they rode back up to the first floor where he lived. He was whistling, and it struck her that he was happy.

They Go There Forever

He was outside her house. He knocked on the door. She invited him in. He stood with his hat in his hand. She asked for it. He examined the room. It was a small outer chamber, somewhat formal in its appointment, elaborately decorated, high cornices and wainscotting. He began to grow warmer as the room grew familiar. He examined each corner. It grew larger and larger. He came to a doorway. Beyond this room was another room. He passed through the opening, following her inward. Beyond this room was another room. He followed her forward. They went inward together, deeper and deeper. Beyond this room was another room, both smaller and larger, more than familiar, and beyond this is another room. They go there forever.

The Happy Object

Once upon a time there was an object which made everyone happy. You can imagine how happy it felt.

The Dissatisfied Chickens

Once there were some chickens who were dissatisfied with their lot. One day when the woman came into the pen to tend to them one of the chickens grabbed her and pulled her to his naked lap with lascivious intentions. She extricated herself and then heard all the chickens complain. They had lusts, just like people. They wanted the same rights as people. These were mainly sexual rights. They didn't wish to be considered crass by the lady of the house even though they were naked and she wore white. All were unhappy, even the young stunted one with three arms. "But," the woman reasoned, "if you become people you'll lose your egg laying abilities!" However, they didn't give two cents for their egg laying abilities.

The Tale of a Dog

They had gotten the dog on their wedding day as a tiny puppy. As she told it, he had wanted a dog to play ball with, but as he told it, it had been her idea to get a dog so she could lavish her affection on it instead of him. It is said that couples, when they have been together for a while, begin to resemble each other, and after a while perhaps they did, because as they came to hate themselves more and more, as most people do under the pressure of life's cumulative failures, they each decided it was the other whom they hated and he precipitously left, leaving her with the dog.

Dogs, also, are said to come to resemble their owners after a number of years, and every time she looked at the dog now she was reminded of him, and while she didn't mean to neglect the dog, avoiding him became a lot easier than looking him in the muzzle. She wanted *him* to take the dog, now—it was his dog, too, and he had to take some responsibility. But he had a new wife now, and a new puppy, and when he brought the dog to his house on alternate weekends the dog would either attack the new puppy or sulk all day in the dog house. Then *she* remarried and *she* got a new puppy, and when the old dog was shuttled back to her house he usually found a way to quietly let himself out the back gate. When asked, she said he had become quite independent and mature, and was a real role model for her young pup.

He spent most of his days hanging out at the mall, now, and one day when he came back, she said, "Okay, you don't have to stay here anymore at all if you don't want to," and he made his way off into the world. Only occasionally, now, did either of his original owners check in with him. They each thought the other was taking the responsibility for him, anyway. He wandered through the world, taking scraps and living minimally, without any real plans, hopes, or dreams. When asked, his original owners either blamed each other for his aimless state, or blamed him for changing from the physical embodiment of their original love to a huge hairy embarrassment.

One day the woman heard that he had moved in with an old bitch on the other side of town. The woman didn't know why he should want to do that. The bitch was old enough to be his mother.

From the Window

The mountains have come back after a long vacation from the window.

We Will Never Return Here Again

This is a picture of some very pretty flowers, but you can't tell from this picture how pretty they are.

This is a picture of a most remarkable tree, but this picture doesn't do it justice. You can't tell by looking at this picture how remarkable the tree was.

There is a bug in this picture, an incredible bug. But it's blurry. You can't see it.

There are panoramic views all the way around. This is only one of them. And you can't tell by looking at this picture how large the ocean is, how heavy the air is, how the sound of the wind in the plumeria is missing, just like rain.

We will never return here again.

A History Of Abuse

Once there was an exquisite pussycat who became engaged to marry a real dog. She broke it off twice. The idea of sex with him was disgusting. You try to picture it. But in the end, she married him. He had squirreled away bones all over the yard, and that's what impressed her, who carefully buried each treasure which came out from under her tail. The explanation that she offered for this was that she had lived through the Depression.

Still, she remained depressed, especially after the kitten came. Of course, it wasn't a real kitten. It was half dog. And to her, it was all dog. To the dog, however, it was only less than cat.

Like her father, the pup-kit was loyal. Her father would never be disloyal to her mother, even when she spat at him. Even when she went catting around and didn't come home until the wee hours of the morning. Only when the dog got up to start his day of squirreling now did the cat come to bed. But the dog couldn't be annoyed with her—after all, she was nocturnal and he was not.

He knew he couldn't expect her to be loyal to him. If he was loyal to her it wasn't because he was more virtuous—it was just because he was a dog. He couldn't stop himself from being loyal. This was just how God had made him, and every day he thanked God for making him the way he was. The cat, on the other hand, thanked God every day for making her a cat.

The pup-kit didn't know what to thank God for, and so she didn't thank Him. Perhaps this was when the trouble started.

The pup-kit wanted to cat around like her mother. But the dog in her chose one mate to be loyal to for life. The dog in her found a mate who would despise her as a dog should be despised. In this way, she earned the scorn of both parents. It was a form of attention.

But one day she woke up as if from a dream and she saw that the mate whom she worshipped was sexually abusing their little girl. She could tell, because she saw that the little pink thing still lying on her back had a sausage-like penis sticking out of her. Nausea overcame her as she realized that not only was it impossible for her to stop this from happening, she herself was responsible for this horror.

Food or Mirrors

There are endless preparations for the big event which will eventually take place in a room without food or mirrors.

For the Camera

He liked to take pictures. He liked to be in the pictures. He liked to have the pictures as a record that he lived his life. These pictures told a story—the story of the life of which they were the proof.

A Dog's Death

Once there was a young couple who didn't really love each other. They decided to get a dog.

They didn't really decide, of course. Nature decided. Society decided. If one was married, one had a dog.

The woman read up on all sorts of dogs. She looked in the newspaper. Dogs cost a lot of money. She decided to go to the pound.

But on the way to the pound, she stopped at the supermarket, because if one was married, one had to eat. If one was married, one had to go to the supermarket. Perhaps the woman didn't exactly love her husband. Still, she went to the supermarket.

There was an angel giving away a puppy in front of the supermarket. A good angel or a bad angel—the woman couldn't be sure. Or maybe it was just a woman like herself.

"How much?" the woman asked.

"You can have him for free," the angel said. "Look at his paws. He's not going to be very big. Small to medium."

So the woman took him home. So now they had a dog, and the woman quickly trained her husband to take him outside when he wanted to go. However, in the daytime the husband went to work and the woman had to take him outside. At first, she resented this bitterly. Then she began to enjoy sitting on the back step and watching him go. She, of course, had to clean up his poop, and so she began to love the thing, in a way, because we always love what we have to clean up the poop of.

They named the pooch Sherril, and he started to grow. It began to annoy the woman, now, that wherever she went with her dog people would say, "Is that really Sherril? What are you feeding him? Look at his paws! Have you ever seen paws that big?"

Sometimes at night the woman would say to her husband, "Isn't Sherril a great dog!" ashamed because she was sure Sherril was way too big, much bigger than other people's dogs.

Sherril was always asking to go out, now, and the woman let him go, hoping he would poop on someone else's lawn. Sometimes he would come back full of mud. Then the woman would have to wash him and put him to bed.

He was too big for his bed. He oozed out of it, and his head rested on the floor. A great sigh came out of him. The woman sat drinking her coffee wondering if in some way Sherril wasn't some terrible mistake.

Everyone in the neighborhood loved Sherril, and the woman had a harder and harder time getting him to come in the house. She called and called, but he ran away, ran across the street and under a hedge.

So the woman went in the house alone. After a while, a child from down the street came to the door and said that Sherril had been hit by a car. He was around the corner on a busy street where the woman thought he never would go. The woman raced.

Cars were pulled up all around him. A crowd of people surrounded him. "Let me through!" the woman screamed. Blood poured from him. His muzzle was crushed. "He's still alive!" someone said.

They helped her lift him into the car. She couldn't do it alone. On the way to the vet, Sherril let out a howl. The woman began screaming.

At the vet they said they didn't know whether he would live. Both his hips were broken. He was bleeding inside. His muzzle was crushed. If he lived, his brain might be damaged. He might not be able to walk. It was going to cost a lot of money.

The woman sat in the waiting room and the tears poured out of her. She hadn't known she loved this dog so deeply.

When he died, her grief came down like iron bars around her.

Viola da Gamba

Anita found all the guys in their group attractive for one reason or another—Paul's South American moustache was very sexy, Barry's encounters with vampires on the London underground were very romantic, and Raymond's reasonable intelligence was also not without appeal. She would have been glad had any of them chosen her to be his girlfriend. However, the guy who did choose her was Dave, the guy she hardly dared hope for. He wasn't just another guy—he was her father.

Dave, of course, was older than the other guys, and had a lot more savoir faire, and when he rubbed himself against Anita she felt some of his prestige rub off on her. Still, she was insecure when she was with him, and sometimes she would get very anxious that someone would find out that they were living together. She knew they were living in sin. That was why she married him.

Anita's life with Dave wasn't easy. He was very authoritarian and sometimes barked like a dog at her if she came home late after being out with a girlfriend. He, on the other hand, often stayed out until very late while Anita sat in the dark, smoking, wondering if he was out with one of her sisters. Indeed, Anita's pain was so deep that she thanked God every day for giving her a man worth so much suffering.

Anita was still in school, and one day her art teacher told her to sketch her own feet for homework. This she had to do in front of a mirror, and so she brought her sketch pad and pencils into her dressing room and sat down to work with her feet up against the mirror. She had put on her favorite shoes, the shoes a gay Parisienne might have worn. Her ankles looked very pretty, her shoes in the mirror looked very gay. Thus she sat, drawing happily, looking only at her feet in the mirror. She didn't dare to look at the rest of herself. She was afraid of what she would see.

When she was done, she stood up and walked into the bedroom, which was lit with a gray light. The television was on. Dave was sitting on the bed. Of course, he had finished school long ago, and didn't have any homework. Dave's face was grey. There were pouches under his eyes. He had a neck like a turkey.

Time passed. Waves began to wash over Anita. Each wave was a wish—a wish to have a baby. But how could she have babies with Dave? They would turn out blind and insane.

So she stopped smoking. She said to herself—"I am a non-smoker. I have never smoked. I don't know how to hold a cigarette." A pregnant woman musn't smoke. Smoking could damage a fetus. "I don't smoke," she told Dave. "Yes you do," he said, smoking.

Lightning struck the tower. It began to burn, and then to explode. Dave flew off in one direction and Anita in the other.

She wasn't hurt, she thought. Only on Father's Day now, she felt blue. Dave stopped her on the street. She turned and ran the other way. "You can't do this!" he yelled after her. "I made you!"

Printed November 1989 in Santa Barbara & Ann Arbor
for the Black Sparrow Press by Graham Mackintosh
& Edwards Brothers Inc. Design by Barbara Martin.
This edition is published in paper wrappers; there
are 250 hardcover trade copies; 100 copies have
been numbered & signed by the author; & 26 lettered
copies have been handbound in boards by Earle Gray,
each with an original drawing by Sherril Jaffe.

Photo credit: Ronnie Buchman

Sherril Jaffe lives in the Hudson Valley with her husband, Rabbi Alan Lew, and their two children, Hannah and Malka.

Jennifer Melissa Demelza
Arnold Skov